A MERRY CHRISTMAS

ELIZABETH JOHNS

CHAPTER 1

*J*oshua Fielding had always loved Christmas-tide. Even during those long years on campaign against Napoleon, when days were counted not by the calendar but by the movements of the army and the supply of powder, the weeks of Advent had pressed upon him with a peculiar ache. In December he would think of the glow of candlelight in frosted windows, of the scent of plum pudding steaming in his mother's kitchen, of the sound of his father's laugh as he attempted to sing the bass line of a carol. Other soldiers pined for sweethearts left behind. Joshua pined for the merry chaos of his own family.

His family always celebrated in a boisterous fashion that would, in all likelihood, appal his aristocratic colleagues. Yet he loved it. His father had built a shipping empire and operated out of both Liverpool and London, but their country estate was nestled somewhat in between, in the idyllic setting of the Cotswold countryside.

The elder Mr. Fielding's partner, Mr. Roxton, had grown equally prosperous, and the two families had long since entwined their Christmas celebrations into one annual carnival of noise and conviviality. That mingling of households was as much a fixture of the season as holly in the hall or the great yule-log laid upon the hearth.

It had been five years since Joshua had been home for a family Christmas...five years in which he had learned how quickly a man's innocence could be traded for the smell of powder and the sight of blood. The boy who had left in new regimentals had returned a captain, older in countenance than in years, and carrying a silence in his thoughts that he could not yet name.

As he approached the village, he halted his gelding to appreciate the story-book view: thatched cottages in a row, with their honeyed limestone, the smell of wood burning, and the smoke escaping the chimneys. The leaves were long gone, but it did not distract from the picturesque scene as frost glistened off the branches from the setting sun's last rays.

He urged Brutus forward. It was quite cold and the air took on the smell just before snow fell. He did not know if there was such a thing, but he would swear it was so.

Somehow he no longer belonged in the simple, innocent settings, tainted as he was by war and bloodshed. Yet he craved it. The only thing he dreaded was his mother's matchmaking. Would she have forsaken him by now?

Joshua was one of six; he fondly remembered their loud and lively gatherings. All his siblings had married and had children, so he expected the volume to be enough to lift the roof off the manor-house's rafters. Would the Roxton family be there as well? He rode on into the quiet village; most country folk would have finished work and be sitting down to their supper by now. He had told his family to expect him, but not to delay a meal for him.

As he turned into the gates of Wychwood Hall, he was welcomed by the tall evergreens lining the drive. Inhaling deeply, the deep juniper scent was one of the fragrances that always reminded him of home. When the house finally came into view, it was a welcoming sight as candles brightened the windows.

A groom came out to take his horse, and as Joshua stood at the front door, graced with a wreath of holly, he smiled, for he could hear his family within. He did not bother to knock as he doubted it would be heard.

A crowd of merrymakers was the best description he could offer as he looked into the drawing room, full of adults and children alive with talk and laughter. They must have waited for him. He recognized some of the children, but not all, and the Roxton family and their brood appeared to be present.

"Joshua!" his mother exclaimed, being the first to see him. She hurried towards him with open arms and met him with a warm embrace. That was soon followed by each and every member of his family.

"I told him you would be here in time," his brother, Simon, proclaimed.

"You should not have waited for me. Please go on ahead and I will be down as soon as I have made myself presentable."

"Very well," his father agreed. Joshua went upstairs to find a servant unpacking his saddle-bag.

By the time he returned, they were almost all seated. Whilst the adults sat at the very large table in the dining room, on special occasions another table was brought in for the children in an adjoining salon, opened up so they might all eat together.

He looked around and found the only remaining seat, which was between his mother and what must be one of the Roxton girls, who was now no longer a girl. Her auburn hair was arranged in elegant coils above a gown of deep green satin that set off a complexion like fresh cream, and yet something in the turn of her head seemed... familiar.

Perhaps this was his mother's latest effort at matchmaking, he mused. Now he had to remember which one she was before he embarrassed himself.

There was Meredith—Merry—as she had always been called, who had been about fourteen when last he'd seen her, and could have been mistaken for a boy were it not for the two plaits she had worn. She had constantly plagued him and his brothers, wanting to best them at everything. But that young girl had been freckled and plain, and could not be this beauty before him.

The only other Roxton girl, Penelope, was a little older, but he thought he recalled his mother mentioning that she had married. That meant…he looked up and as if his mother understood his dilemma, she mouthed, 'Merry.' Then she turned to her other dinner partner on her left, leaving him to muddle through the awkwardness.

'Twas impossible this young lady could be… "Good evening, Merry."

"Captain," she returned. A footman placed a bowl of his favourite oxtail soup before him. His stomach growled with both appreciation and anticipation. It had been over six hours since he last stopped for a meal. "You did not recognize me, did you?"

Joshua paused as he was about to take a spoonful. He set down his spoon and looked at her. As he took in her auburn locks and pale green eyes, he noticed the barest hint of freckles dusting her nose and cheeks. The mischievous twinkle in her eyes—that understood precisely—seemed to dare him to be honest.

"No, I did not."

"Without plaits and freckles, it is difficult, I am sure."

"I had but to hear you speak," he retorted. That sharp tongue of hers was unmistakable.

She laughed, a deep melodious sound that did something strange to his insides. No, that was his stomach, reminding him how long it had been since he'd eaten his favourite soup. He picked up his spoon and dipped it into the bowl of savoury broth.

They dined well. Roast goose, crisp-skinned and fragrant with sage; baked apples stuffed with raisins and almonds; carrots glazed in butter, and a haunch of venison from the neighbouring estate. Conversation flowed easily around him—news of mutual acquaintances, comments on the frost promising a skating party on Boxing Day, mild complaints about the scarcity of good apples this year.

He had almost begun to relax when Merry, in a tone of idle curiosity, asked, "Is it true you are attached to a secret troop in the army?"

Joshua nearly sent his wine across the table. He sputtered and coughed all the same. "Where did you hear such a thing?"

Her smile suggested she believed not a word of his deflection. "I did not hear it, I deduced it. And your reaction confirms it."

Joshua cursed to himself. She was correct—his reaction had not been professional. Why was this little sprite setting him so at odds? Granted, she was not so little anymore, but the mischief definitely still resided within her.

"I belong to a troop that often performs special services for the Crown. I hardly make a secret of that."

"As you say," she replied with a tone that did not imply she was convinced.

"That is neither here nor there. I am on holiday and do not intend to work while I am here."

She sighed with long suffering. "I hope that does not mean you will refuse to speak of your adventures. You are well aware, are you not, that we will be thrust together every moment the families are gathered together?"

He wrinkled his brow and turned to her, considering what she had said, which must have been mistaken for misunderstanding, for she waved her hand in a circle for him to examine their surroundings.

"We are the only two unmarried," she pointed out, as if to a simpleton. "Naturally, we will be paired together."

He did not reply. Thankfully, the present course was removed and the next laid out. It was time for him to speak to his mother on his other side, but apparently Merry had other ideas, since she continued:

"That is, unless Tremaine is invited."

Joshua was filled with dread. He had hoped not to hear that name while he was home, if ever again.

"Why would Tremaine be invited?" He had been the bane of Joshua's childhood existence. Always competing. Bullying him. The cit's son and the lord of the manor's—a natural rivalry, many would say.

"He has been courting me. Father expects him to make an offer soon."

The forkful of cod in Joshua's mouth turned to ash. Had she no idea what kind of man Tremaine was? How did her family allow it?

Joshua knew some response was required, but what could he say that would neither condemn nor condone? He had no right. He had not been a part of Merry's life in years and would leave soon and have little to do with her in the future.

"He must have changed a great deal, then," he heard himself say.

"What do you infer?"

Joshua realized he had badly erred. He did not possess the smooth tongue of his friend, Ashley Stuart. "I have yet to hear that tigers change their stripes, and Tremaine was a rogue of the worst kind."

Instead of shaking in horror at his words, her expression challenged him. "Is that so? Are you implying that his intentions toward me are not honourable?"

"How could I know what his intentions are? I can only speak with a surety that Tremaine only does what benefits him."

He made the mistake of looking her in the eye. Those green eyes had deepened to emerald and were shooting daggers at him. "You think he only wants my fortune." It was not a question.

Joshua was certain of that, but Merry was also beautiful. Yet the aristocracy did not normally make honourable offers to the daughters of cits. He pondered how to answer, but again she challenged him first.

"If that is the case, then prove it."

He had not been home two hours and had already dug himself into a hole with no escape. He picked up his glass of wine and took a long drink. "If that is the case, then it shall not be too difficult. If not, then I shall wish you joy."

She picked up her glass and clinked it against his. "I shall look forward to it."

CHRISTMAS WAS Merry's favourite time of the year, most likely because of her name. The other reason was that she loved the big family gatherings with the Fielding family. Now that everyone else had married, she often felt lonely.

She was soon to be one and twenty, and despite being quite wealthy, her parents would never hear of giving her a London Season.

Their hard-earned money was not good enough for the nobs in London, her father always said.

Merry had accepted their decision with as much grace as she could, but certainly had had no prospects in their sleepy corner of the Cotswolds—until recently.

Lord Bruton had a country estate there, but other than some elderly spinster aunts, rarely did the family occupy it these days. When they decided to spend their holiday there this year, you would have thought the king and queen were coming for a visit. It had spread amongst the villagers faster than fire on dry straw.

Merry had little hope of anything coming of it, but it was hard not to be excited at something happening in the neighbourhood for once; that and the Fielding and Roxton siblings returning for their large festive gathering. When Lord Bruton and family had arrived to fill the always-empty pew at the front of the church, the entire congregation was aflutter. Merry had been entirely amused by the situation until she'd turned and seen the dark, handsome visage of the Honourable Barnaby Tremaine. Then, despite herself, she was all aflutter too. When he'd cast glances at her during the service, she'd felt a little breathless.

Afterwards, when they had been introduced, she had thought she might melt into a puddle when he kissed the air above her hand. She had become, in fact, a cliché that she had always made fun of. Thankfully, she had not swooned. The indignity!

Her family would never call on his, or vice versa, so when they met again, it was on the village High Street, at the house of mutual acquaintances, or at the village assembly, where he singled her out and danced with her twice. His attention towards her had been most marked, even to a practical girl like Merry who was not wont to have her head turned by a handsome face or elegantly tied neckcloth.

Nonetheless, even her sceptical father had to begrudgingly acknowledge that the Baron's son was courting her, though he had not been asked to do so, as was proper. Her mother would never say so, but Merry knew she despaired of her daughter finding a suitable mate. The past fortnight had been a fairy tale, and now Joshua Fielding had arrived and threatened to ruin it all.

Joshua Fielding, who had been her first adolescent puppy love, yet had never been more than annoyed by her ploys to get his attention.

He had not been home for years—years—then reappeared as a dashing, handsome war hero and threatened to ruin her only chance at marriage. Her ire rose with each successive thought.

If her father did not object to Tremaine, then how could Captain Fielding?

"Penny for your thoughts?"

Merry forced a smile. She had completely ignored Captain Fielding for her own thoughts.

"Not at all. I was considering all the lovely gestures Mr. Tremaine has made towards me these past weeks, and how contrary they are to your opinion of his character."

"Indeed. Has he spoken to your father, then?"

Curse her blushing cheeks! "Not yet, but he has hinted at his intention to do so."

The insolent man raised one sceptical eyebrow at her. How did he do that?

"What are you two speaking of?" Mrs. Fielding asked.

"Merry was just informing me of her suitor."

Mrs. Fielding frowned. "Do you mean Mr. Tremaine? Has he spoken to your father?"

"Not yet, ma'am."

"Well, then," she said, seeming pleased, "I need not worry that I did not invite him to dinner."

"I imagine he feels no slight," she replied.

"I think we should have dancing tonight. You still remember how to dance, do you not, Joshua?" she asked, moving on from the topic of Barnaby Tremaine.

"It is often required of the King's men. I would not embarrass you, I assure you."

"Well, one hears of such things, but you have not been here for me to know one way or the other."

"You know I would have been here had I been able," he said softly to his mother, and Merry melted towards him a little with his gentle tone towards Mrs. Fielding. A very little. She was still rather cross with his defamation of Mr. Tremaine's character.

"My son, you may show us the waltz that is still forbidden by our rigid vicar. I hear it is beautiful to watch."

Merry had read about the waltz and longed to try it. She had even practised the steps. But to dance it with him? Her stomach churned at the thought.

From the look on Mrs. Fielding's face, Merry knew any objections would be fruitless.

As a rule, their dances were very jovial and lively—nothing at all the way she expected the waltz to be. Perhaps someone else would object, and she would be able to avoid it.

"Why have you not yet married and set up your nursery, Joshua?" Simon, one of the brothers, asked from across the table with a gleam in his eye. It was just the sort of thing Merry would have expected one of the mothers to ask, but the brothers did like to tease.

"From what I can see, the nursery is already full enough." He seemed undisturbed by the taunt.

"Do not tell me you intend to abstain from marital bliss and fatherhood?" Simon continued.

"Matrimony is not well suited with my profession," he argued.

"Yet I read recently of Major Stuart's recent nuptials."

The entire table seemed to have ceased speaking in order to listen. Merry almost felt sorry for him.

"His bride happens to be rather an exception to the traditional sort of lady."

The table looked at him, waiting for further explanation. He did not look inclined to elaborate.

"And what sort of lady is she?" she prompted.

"A rather extraordinary one. She seems to enjoy adventure rather than embroidery and afternoon tea with other ladies. There is nothing at all wrong with either; it is just that most ladies would not tolerate the unusual lifestyle required being married to a military man."

Merry rather thought she'd like to meet Mrs. Stuart. She was not certain she wanted to have a traditional marriage herself, when he described the alternative.

"Perhaps you will find one such as she," his mother said with a gentle pat on his arm as if he needed to be consoled. Merry bit back a grin.

"I assure you I am quite content, Mother."

A look crossed Mrs. Fielding's face that spoke sympathy, perhaps even pity, as though she thought him misguided.

"Now you have bungled matters, Brother. All the ladies here will be on their mettle to prove you wrong!"

"Perhaps their attentions would be best served by aiding Merry, who actually wishes for help," Captain Fielding suggested with a straight face.

How could he say such a thing? She stamped on his foot under the table and was sorely tempted to toss her wine in his face. She cast him a look of disapproval, which was rewarded with a devilish grin. He was enjoying this!

The others began their conversations again, thankfully, and the attention was no longer upon her.

"Am I wrong?" he asked. "You just waxed eloquently about Mr. Tremaine and his courtship."

"Not entirely, but I do not need the help, as it were, of the collective families!" she growled. "It was ungentlemanly of you."

"Then I beg your pardon," he responded in a tone that belied his words.

CHAPTER 2

The next morning, Joshua woke before the rest of the household. It was a habit too firmly ingrained by years of military discipline to be easily shaken—and truthfully, it was a welcome moment of solitude before the day's noise began. The fire in his chamber had burned low, but a faint glow of embers gave enough warmth for him to dress without haste.

He washed in cold water, shrugged into his coat, and made his way downstairs. The house was quiet but for the faint creak of timbers and the distant clatter of the kitchen. Halfway down the main staircase, a warm, rich fragrance reached him—spices, sugar, and butter: the unmistakable scent of Christmas baking.

He slowed his step, drinking it in. How many times had he woken to just such a scent in this house as a boy? In those days, the thought of currant buns fresh from the oven or mince pies cooling on wire racks had been enough to lure him into the kitchen before the cook was ready for visitors. Some things, it seemed, did not change.

The baize door to the kitchen passage was ajar. Joshua stepped through, and the warmth hit him in a wave. The great kitchen hearth roared with heat as copper pots hung gleaming from their hooks and every surface seemed laden with some stage of preparation—trays of ginger cake cut into slices; ribbons of pastry laid out for tarts; great bowls of dried fruit waiting to be stirred into the plum puddings.

And there, at the far table, stood Merry. Her sleeves were rolled to the elbow over a dark blue wool gown, and a plain white apron was tied neatly at her waist. A wisp of auburn hair had escaped its pins to curl against her cheek, and she was bent over a hamper, arranging jars and parcels in orderly layers.

Joshua paused in the doorway. For a moment, the image was so domestic—so utterly unlike the self-assured young lady sparring with him at last night's dinner—that he found himself oddly reluctant to break it.

She glanced up and caught him hesitating. "You are abroad early, Captain. I thought soldiers relished the chance to lie abed when not on campaign."

"Some of us are past saving," he replied, stepping into the room. "Though I might have stayed abed if I had known the scent of your baking would reach even the top floor. What treacherous inducement is this?"

"My baking?" She laughed, shaking her head. "I am merely conscripted to help pack the Christmas hampers. The cook and kitchen maids have done all the clever work. I am the common labour."

Joshua came closer, glancing at the contents of the nearest basket. "Common? That looks to me like the work of a quartermaster—everything fitted to the inch. Bread, cheese, jars of jam, apples…and is that a joint of beef beneath the cloth?"

"It is. One for each of our tenants, along with candles, dried beans, and some sweetmeats for the children. The Roxtons and Fieldings have been doing this together since before I was born."

"I remember." He smiled faintly. "When we were children, I always tried to arrange it so I would be the one to hand over the ginger cake, thinking it would earn me extra thanks."

"And did it?"

"Only from the ones under ten. Their parents generally thanked my mother."

The door swung open, admitting Mrs. Fielding and Mrs. Roxton, both wrapped in shawls despite the kitchen's heat.

"There you are, Joshua," his mother said with satisfaction, as though she had been hoping to find him here. "Merry has nearly finished packing the last of the hampers. We thought you might be the one to drive her about to deliver them."

Joshua glanced at Merry, whose expression was carefully neutral. "Is that so?"

"It will save the grooms the trouble," Mrs. Roxton added, entirely too innocently. "And you know the tenants—they will be glad to see you both."

He might have objected—but two pairs of maternal eyes were fixed upon him in expectation, and he had faced down less daunting odds in battle. "Very well," he said, with a slight bow. "If Miss Roxton feels able to endure my company for the morning."

Merry gave a little curtsy, her tone perfectly polite. "If Captain Fielding is certain the task will not prove too dull after his… adventures."

He smiled knowingly, enjoying her verbal sparring, despite them both knowing full well their mothers were throwing them together for a purpose.

They finished packing the last two hampers together, side by side at the table. Joshua found it impossible not to notice the faint scent of lavender water clinging to her despite the kitchen aromas.

By the time they carried the baskets out to the courtyard, the pale winter sun had risen over the frosted hedgerows. A light dusting of snow had fallen in the night, just enough to whiten the gravel. The family's cart was waiting, harnessed to a sturdy bay cob, his breath steaming in the air.

Two of Joshua's nephews came pelting out as they were loading the baskets. "Uncle Joshua, may we come?" cried Roger, his cheeks scarlet from the cold.

"Not today," Joshua said, lifting him onto the cart's step so he could peer in at the hampers. "You would eat half the sweetmeats before they reached the tenants."

"I would not!" Roger protested hotly—then spoiled the effect by snatching a candied plum from the top of one parcel and popping it in his mouth.

Merry laughed, ruffling the boy's hair. "We will bring you back something from Mrs. Hobson's kitchen if you let us go in peace."

That promise was enough to send both boys racing back into the house, calling for plum cake.

They set out at a steady trot, the wheels crunching softly over the snowy lane. The air was sharp and bright, the fields on either side lying in winter sleep beneath a silver veil of frost. Joshua took the reins easily—it was the first time in years he had driven along these roads, yet every turn was as familiar as the lines on his own palm.

At the first cottage, a white-haired woman opened the door even before they knocked. "Well, if it is not Miss Merry and young Master Joshua!" she exclaimed, beaming. "Come in, come in, you will freeze out there."

They left her with the hamper and a promise of carols on Christmas Eve. At the second, they were mobbed by three children in patched coats who all wanted to carry something in. Merry crouched to their level, producing a packet of sugar biscuits tied in red ribbon. "One each, mind you," she said, in the tone of someone well-accustomed to enforcing fairness.

At the third cottage, a thin man with a cough accepted the hamper with quiet gratitude. Joshua remembered his face—he had been a younger man when Joshua had last seen him, hale and broad-shouldered. Time and hardship had pared him down. Joshua pressed a crown into his hand, murmuring something about it being from the King's army, and the man's eyes brightened.

By the time they had made their way along the outer lane and back toward the village, Merry's cheeks were pink from the cold and her breath clouded in the air. Yet she had not once complained, and her cheer seemed to warm each doorstep they visited.

"You are good at this," Joshua said as they turned toward the High Street.

"At what?"

"Making people feel they matter. You know every name, and half their stories."

"It is hardly difficult when you have lived here all your life," she said lightly. "Besides, people do matter. And at Christmas most of all."

He glanced at her, but she was looking ahead, her profile calm in the winter light.

"Indeed."

MERRY HAD AWOKEN with the particular cheer which belonged to Christmas week and to work that promised usefulness. Long before most of the house had stirred, she had slipped from her room, coaxed her hair into something like order, and gone down to the kitchen, there to marshal jars, parcels, and papered packets into neat tiers within wicker hampers. She liked the arithmetic of it: two loaves, a cut of beef, a round of cheese, a pot of jam, candles, beans, and a bundle of comfits tied up with red ribbon for small hands. It pleased her to think of those hands untying the bow.

When Captain Fielding appeared at the kitchen door—fair from the cold, fair in himself, and all the more striking for the plainness of his coat—she had schooled her countenance to composure. If her heart had executed a small and ridiculous leap, no one need suspect it. He had that soldier's way of taking in a room at once, and then fastening upon the work to be done as if it were no matter. She was not sorry his mother and hers had contrived that they should deliver the hampers together—she was only sorry for his choosing last evening to imply he might extract her from a danger that did not exist.

The morning had been brisk and busy. At each cottage Joshua had lifted the heavier parcels without flourish, and with a gravity which made thanks easier to offer. He remembered people, too. Not merely faces, but histories: a cow gone barren the year of the bad hay...a son taken to sea...a girl now out at service in Stow. It was unaccountably soothing.

By the time they turned in to the High Street, the sun was a pale coin above the church tower, and the little world of the village was awake. Smoke rose in steady columns, shopkeepers swept their thresholds, and a boy led a stubborn pig past the green with the seriousness of a general before a siege. As they passed the baker's door, warm clouds of spice and yeast wafted to their appreciative noses. The milliner's windows bewitched with velvet and feathers for last-minute Christmas gifts. Children skated their boots upon the clear patches of ice as if the lane were a ballroom polished for their capers. Merry loved it all.

"Mrs. Hobson will scold if we are ten minutes late," she said, knowing already that Mrs. Hobson would scold even if they were ten minutes early.

"Then we must face our punishment," Captain Fielding returned, with that dry civility which somehow made her smile.

The door to the bakery let out a rush of sweet, yeasty air. Mrs. Hobson herself came bustling out, flour on her apron. "You have missed my currant buns by ten minutes," she scolded fondly. "But I have some seed cake that will do for a treat to warm you, with a cup of cider."

As they left the bakery, the distinctive sound of well-sprung wheels and rhythmic clatter of hooves came up behind them. She knew she would see a curricle before she turned her head—perhaps she had been listening for it all morning. Its harness gleamed while its tiger sat with professional insolence, and its master handled the ribbons with a confidence that drew the eye.

Mr. Barnaby Tremaine was very handsome. She was not disposed to be ungrateful to Providence for the fact. He had the sort of dark comeliness that milliners fashioned upon their mannequins when they wished to sell cravats. His hair was as glossy as a rook's wing, his eyes a bold brown, and his mouth given to an insolent smile. His attire projected the London gentleman, with his coat of the newest cut, his gloves the finest kid, and his boots glossed to a mirror-like shine. Where Captain Fielding was all function turned into grace—broad of shoulder without heaviness, lean and quick, his fair hair cropped close as if he still expected to wear a shako—Mr. Tremaine was grace made into a function: a creature designed for drawing rooms, card tables, and the admiration of those who confused expense with taste.

He pulled up just short of the cart and sprang down with elegant ease. "Miss Roxton," he said, bowing over her hand in a manner calculated to create a small spectacle of the exercise. "If Christmas means angels abroad upon the earth, then I see we are properly observed."

Merry might have laughed if the speech had been less pleased with itself. "Good morning, Mr. Tremaine. You are abroad very early for a gentleman who does not rise without the promise of a view in the mirror."

That made him laugh in earnest. He clearly liked impertinence when it came from pretty lips. "Cruelty, Miss Roxton, before noon?" He turned, the bow to the Captain becoming the spare salutation of one man to another when there is history neither will set out before a crowd. "I had not understood you were returned, Fielding."

"Only yesterday," Captain Fielding said. His smile, if it could be called such, was the very minimum demanded by civility. "We are delivering hampers."

"So I perceive. Charity and beef. I applaud the ancient usages. For my small part, I bring nothing but idleness and a long morning before me. Might I steal Miss Roxton from her labours for a turn along the street? I promise to return her before you can miss her."

Merry's pulse—the unmanageable traitor—gave a flutter wholly disproportionate to the request. She opened her mouth to make some neat acceptance, and then shut it again, for Captain Fielding had not removed his hand from the reins, and the line of his profile suggested that he did not intend to do so.

"We have yet two households on the lane," he said. "Mr. Piper, and the widow Fryer."

Tremaine looked as if he would have liked to argue with the order of the universe, but the tiger coughed, the horses stamped, and two of Mrs. Hobson's little apprentices came out to stare with eyes the size of pennies. He adjusted his gloves instead. "Then I shall accompany you.

It is the least I can do, to witness such virtues. I shall carry a hamper, if it will make me useful."

Merry saw, with painful clarity, that what Captain Fielding would most like to carry was Mr. Tremaine and set him down at the far end of the county. She saw also that they were three people in a very small patch of winter sunlight, and that the village was always grateful for a show. She smiled, as if such a morning ought always to include a gentleman or two hovering about a cart of good deeds.

"If you carry a hamper, sir," she said, "you will carry it without sampling."

"Miss Roxton," he protested, hand to heart, "you wrong me. I have never sampled anything I did not intend to purchase."

"Then it is a good thing these are not for sale."

Captain Fielding's mouth moved a fraction—whether in amusement or contempt, she could not say.

At Mr. Piper's, who mended boots and men's patience in equal measure, Tremaine insisted upon carrying in the hamper and upon setting it down where Mrs. Piper did not wish it at all. Captain Fielding quietly lifted it to the proper place without remark. At Widow Fryer's, Tremaine took the lead in describing the excellence of the beef and the plum, as if the season, the Scriptures, and the celebration of the same were his invention, while Captain Fielding stooped to make the fire draw and set the kettle to boil. The widow, who was as sharp as misfortune can make one, thanked Tremaine aloud and Fielding with her eyes, and Merry hoped neither gentleman would be vain enough to require more.

On the way between homes, it was impossible that she should not compare them, for they were as unlike as two gentlemen could be, and yet both charmed. There was strength in the Captain—a breadth across the shoulders that did not require a tailor to proclaim it, hands scarred here and there by work he had done whilst never thinking to preserve them from blemish, and a way of moving that suggested he knew where he was at every moment and what the ground beneath him was doing.

Mr. Tremaine, by contrast, was a picture in a print-shop window

—a very fine one. But there was in him, sometimes, a note of calculation, as though he had learned too exactly how to be desired, and was now impatient at having to perform the lesson again for duller pupils. Was there more to him then, than a pretty shell?

It was not fair to stand them side by side within her mind and declare a prize. They were not horses, and she was not at Tattersall's. She was a sensible girl who had waited a very long time for an excitement of her own, and she would not be dissuaded from tasting it, merely because Captain Fielding chose to remember Tremaine as a bully of the schoolroom. Men changed…boys most of all.

"You are quite silent, Miss Roxton," Tremaine remarked, at the very moment she wished her thoughts were printed somewhere safer than her eyes. "I shall believe I have offended you if you do not abuse me soon."

"I was reckoning how many pies you have not sampled," she said.

"There, you see? Every word an injustice." He bent nearer. "Will you save me two dances on Twelfth Night? I have put my name down upon Miss Lennox's list, but I confess I came upon it with a pencil."

"I save no dances before I have seen the company," she replied. "It is a rule which saves me a world of apologies later."

"Then I shall keep my evening clear of other claims," he said, as if gallantry were the same as possession. Tremaine bowed over her hand after helping her into the cart, then departed.

Captain Fielding said nothing at all—only flicked a glance at the cob's ears and sent the cart forward again.

CHAPTER 3

It was after noon when they turned the cart back into the Wychwood drive. The house stood bright against the pale sky, smoke curling from its chimneys in slow, grey plumes. The bay cob tossed its head, as though knowing the comforts that awaited within. Joshua handed the reins to a groom, swung lightly to the ground, and went to offer his hand to Merry.

She placed her gloved fingers in his, steadying herself as she stepped down. The brief weight of her hand against his palm carried more meaning than he liked. For one thing, it was absurd to notice that her fingers were light, that her balance was sure, and that she looked up at him with eyes half narrowed against the wind and laughing at some private thought. For another, he did not know what to do with the flicker of warmth that such small observations awoke in him. He was a seasoned soldier, not a callow youth to be taking flights of fancy.

The morning had passed with disconcerting ease—ease, that is, until Tremaine had inserted himself into it, as though the man had been summoned to spoil all Joshua had begun to recall with pleasure. He had not minded the hampers, or even Merry's cheerfulness at each cottage door. Indeed, there had been a deep contentment in seeing her received so fondly by everyone, from the blacksmith to the widow at the end of the lane. But Tremaine's sudden appearance had cast a shadow over all. It had reminded him, as though he needed reminding, that she was not the tousle-headed girl who had once pestered him with snowballs, but a woman of one-and-twenty whose future might—without interference—be bound to a man Joshua could never stomach.

She thanked him with formal politeness when her feet touched the gravel, but there was the faintest curve at her mouth that did not feel entirely polite. He could not decide whether it mocked him, or herself, or Tremaine, or the whole absurdity of the morning. Perhaps it was all of those at once.

They carried the empty hampers around toward the kitchen door, and Joshua found himself thinking—not for the first time—that Merry Roxton was dangerous. Not in the manner of cannon or cavalry, which one could meet with drilled composure, but dangerous in the quieter way of a sudden thaw when one expected ice: beautiful, welcome even, and all the more treacherous for being unexpected.

Snow had begun to fall, soft flakes drifting across the courtyard as if to soften the day's sharpness. The sound of laughter drew them onward, and as they rounded the corner they saw a troop of Fielding and Roxton family members gathered in the side garden, cloaks and bonnets pulled close, baskets in hand. The women had resolved to hunt for holly and mistletoe, while the men set themselves to the ancient task of bringing in a yule log large enough to burn until Twelfth Night.

"Uncle Joshua!" cried Roger, Simon's eldest, already red-cheeked from running. "You must come and help! We've found one as big as a cannon!"

"I hope it does not explode," Joshua replied, ruffling the boy's hair. He glanced at Merry, who was stooping to adjust Archie's cloak, her face soft with patience. The sight warmed him against the wind.

Soon enough, he was out with the men, trampling through the copse at the edge of the park. There lay a fallen oak, half buried in snow, which the younger ones declared perfect for the yule log. Ropes were fetched, shoulders bent, and amid much slipping, grunting, and laughter, they heaved the enormous piece of timber onto a makeshift sledge. Joshua found himself laughing with them—real laughter, not the careful amusement he used at table or in town. He had forgotten the satisfaction of common effort, of labour that ended in merriment.

At last they dragged the log to where the ladies admired it, their baskets already brimming with glossy holly and greens. Someone produced a spray of mistletoe tied with a scarlet ribbon, and the children capered about with it, holding it over unsuspecting heads until kisses were claimed amid much mock outrage.

Joshua found himself beside Merry again, both of them catching their breath after the haul. Snow had caught in the dark auburn of her hair, melting in tiny drops. She shook it back with a laugh. "You see? I told you Christmas work was not for the faint-hearted."

"You did not tell me it involved hauling artillery across a field," he returned, and she laughed again, quick and clear, before falling into step with him as they followed the log back to the great hall.

The yule log was set with ceremony in the hearth, the children excited as they watched. Garlands were hung about the mantels, and the room filled with the scent of pine and burning oak. Wine and spiced cakes were passed around, and soon the company dispersed into small knots of conversation, content to enjoy the warmth while the snow thickened beyond the windows.

Joshua had thought to retreat to a corner, but Merry was there before him, carrying a plate of ginger cake. She offered it with the air of one who knows she cannot be refused. "You worked as hard as any," she said. "You have earned a slice."

He accepted, and for a moment they stood together, the noise of family around them, the fire crackling at their backs.

Merry took a modest portion herself and then, without looking at him, asked, "Do you mean to remain long in Gloucestershire, Captain?"

"Until Twelfth Night," he said. "Long enough to enjoy the season, I hope."

"Long enough," she murmured, "to prove me wrong."

He did not answer.

It was she who broke the silence. "I suppose you are still determined to dislike Mr. Tremaine?"

Joshua did not reply at once. He studied the shifting firelight instead. "I am not determined," he said finally, "to see ill where there is none, but until I have cause to believe him changed, I cannot like him for your intended."

"People do change," she said. Her tone was light, but there was an edge beneath. "He is not the boy you knew. None of us are who we were five years ago."

Joshua glanced at her then, and saw in the tilt of her chin that she was daring him to contradict her. "That is true enough," he conceded. "But some men polish themselves like silver until they gleam in the candlelight, and some forge themselves like steel. I will leave it to you to determine what is what."

Her lips pressed together in annoyance, though her eyes glimmered with something more complicated. "And what are you, Captain Fielding? Steel?"

He half smiled. "Rusted, perhaps—and not half so well dressed as Tremaine."

That drew a reluctant laugh from her, though she shook her head as if he were impossible.

Later, when the others had scattered—some to the nursery, some to the card tables—they found themselves once again near the fire, Merry idly twisting a sprig of ivy between her fingers. The noise of the house faded to a murmur. She spoke suddenly, her eyes not on him but on the greenery in her hand.

"Do you have a sweetheart, Captain Fielding?"

The question startled him more than he cared to show. He looked at her steadily, though he felt his heartbeat quicken. "No. The life I have led is not friendly to such luxuries."

Her gaze flicked up then, quick and searching. "Then there has never been anyone? Not even a girl in Spain, or Portugal?"

He shook his head. "There was never time; and perhaps—" He stopped himself, for he had not meant to speak so plainly. "Perhaps I did not wish to bind anyone to uncertainty. Soldiers do not always return."

For a moment she was silent, and he thought he had ended the matter, but then she spoke softly, almost as if to herself. "That is very noble, Captain. Yet even soldiers must have hearts."

He did not answer, because anything he said would be too much, and too soon. Instead he bent his head as though studying the ivy in her hand. "What of you, Merry? Have you already given yours away?"

She coloured, whether with vexation or honesty he could not tell. "That is hardly a question I am bound to answer."

"No," he said, with a trace of a smile, "but you asked me."

Her eyes flashed then, the green deepening. "Perhaps I only wanted to know what sort of man thought he had the right to pronounce upon my suitors. If you had a sweetheart, at least I could forgive you the arrogance. Without one, it seems nothing but presumption."

Joshua felt the sting of the words, but beneath it was a kind of admiration. She was never timid, this Merry. She challenged him as no one else dared. "Then I must hope you will forgive me in time," he said, "for I do not retract my warning."

She regarded him for a long moment, then turned away, placing the sprig of ivy on the mantel. "We shall see, Captain. We shall see."

IF A YOUNG LADY WERE SENSIBLE, she would keep her thoughts in as good order as a basket of coloured thread—every shade in its proper place, untangled. Merry had long suspected she was not that variety of young lady, for the moment she stepped away from Captain Fielding with her bravado still bright upon her tongue—*We shall see, Captain. We shall see*—her thoughts flew up like startled starlings and refused to be coaxed down again.

However, the hall made a picture to soothe any irritation. The yule log, which the gentlemen had brought in with much masculine bustle and grunting, burned at last as if it had found its home in the large hearth. Evergreen garlands were looped along the mantels, ivy adorned every angle, and white-berried mistletoe was wreathed with scarlet ribbon and hung. The air smelt of burning oak and the sort of spice which promised plum pudding in some near future.

"Miss Merry," said Mrs. Fielding, who, with a small silver knife and the inexhaustible calm of a queen, carried a plate of ginger cake, "if you will only take this tray to the music-room, and save us a stampede until after the decorations are finished, I should be most grateful."

"I am all obedience," Merry replied, which made Mrs. Fielding laugh and say something about miracles at Christmas-tide. "As it happens, I was on my way there to put up some decorations."

The music-room had always been her favourite room at Wychwood. Its tall eastern windows were white at the corners now where the snow made lace against the panes, and the pianoforte shone with pampered gloss. Merry set down the tray and took a long breath. The scene in the hall—the heat, the hum, the comfortable confusion—had warmed her body and disordered her mind.

She did not sit. If she sat she would think, and she had not yet decided whether thought was an ally. Instead, she set about laying a short garland of holly around the pianoforte. A little droop at the centre, she mused, two sprigs thrust just so and a narrow ribbon to keep the whole from drooping.

She was engaged in tying the ribbon when Penelope—Mrs. Lennox for some years now—appeared in the doorway with a skein of green twine upon her arm.

"There you are. I told Mama you had not deserted, but she would have it you were setting up a rival wassail in here."

"If I were," Merry said, "it should be better spiced than Papa's."

"Blasphemy," Penelope returned, smiling. "Do you want help?"

"I want five more pairs of hands that understand what I mean without my saying it. You will do admirably." She held out the ribbon's end. "Only here…a little tighter, please."

Penelope obeyed, then studied her sister's face as one studies a sentence for the second meaning it obstinately conceals. "You have been spending much time with Captain Fielding."

"You make it sound as if I had been committing a faux pas or that it was not entirely the machinations of our mother and Mrs. Fielding."

"You always look just a little pleased with yourself after a skirmish," Penelope said.

"Skirmish?" Merry echoed, affecting ignorance, though the word pricked her conscience. She had gone into the fray with her head up and her temper in arms and had come out with neither entirely victorious.

Penelope secured the bow. "He is handsome in the fair way, and he makes me think of iron nails correctly hammered—useful, strong, not to be done without. I suppose that is from being in the army."

"I dare say," Merry said, as if the whole matter were of no consequence at all. "He believes Mr. Tremaine to be a rogue."

"I remember Mr. Tremaine as a boy," Penelope said, her tone the sort people used about the weather—acknowledging what cannot be altered by opinions. "He was very fine at cricket and very poor at truth."

"Perhaps he has mended his ways," Merry said, her voice brisk because it cost her something to say it.

"Yes. Perhaps," Penelope allowed. "Do not take offence, Sister. I am not your enemy."

"My heart is not yet set for or against him."

"You never set your heart against anything but waste."

Merry laughed in spite of herself and kissed her sister's cheek. "That is why I shall not waste this ginger cake. I shall sample it now."

She did, by way of making peace with both Captain Fielding and Mr. Tremaine—for ginger cake was equal in its consolations—and carried the rest back to the hall before there was no more to share.

The house had progressed in her absence from a bustle to a hum. The smallest children had been packed off to the nursery for naps. The older ones had arranged themselves into a society for the betterment of fun and exclaimed at the sight of the ginger cake. Her father, triumphant over his bowl, ladled steaming cups of wassail as if he had invented both drink and ladle. Meanwhile, near the hearth—Merry saw it as one sees rather than looks—Captain Fielding stood and said little while attending to everything.

The children, having exhausted all reasonable amusements indoors, were rapidly turning mutinous. Their mothers, who knew the signs as admirals know storm-clouds, exchanged glances over their tea-cups. The storm would break soon, one way or another.

It was Roger, of course, who declared open rebellion. "There is snow enough for armies!" he cried, nose pressed to the frosted pane. "We must go outside! Uncle Joshua will lead us!"

A chorus rose—pleas, shouts, the rustle of cloaks fetched without permission. Even the younger ones stamped their feet in a parody of marching. Merry, who had been attempting to keep Rose from toppling an inkstand, could not help laughing at the sudden unanimity.

Mrs. Fielding sighed, though her eyes softened. "Very well, only wrap up warmly. And Joshua—" She raised her voice. "—do keep them from burying themselves."

Captain Fielding, who had just returned a tray of cups to the side-board, inclined his head with soldierly obedience, though the faint smile upon his mouth betrayed a man not entirely dismayed by the charge.

Within minutes, boots clattered across flagstones, mufflers were wound, and the hall door burst open. A rush of cold air swept in, along with shrieks of delight as the children poured into the garden, white and glittering in its new coat of snow. Merry followed, tugging her cloak closer. Someone must keep order among the troops, and she did not trust the boys' notions of fairness.

The first volley came from Roger, who packed a ball with all the seriousness of a cannon-shot and let fly at Edmund. It struck him squarely, and war was declared. Children scattered to form battalions. Snow flew, shrieks rang, and the air filled with laughter.

Merry bent quickly, scooped a neat ball, and dispatched it at her nephew, Edmund, who had dared to call her a bystander. The missile landed true, and the child's astonishment was reward enough. "Aunt Merry is with us!" he bellowed, rallying a squadron of five.

"Traitor!" cried another, and suddenly she was very much part of the skirmish.

Snow found her cheek and she gasped. Then she laughed and retaliated in kind. Her gloves were quickly wet through, but she did not care. Years dropped away until she was once more the hoyden of fourteen, pelting any Fielding brother who crossed her path.

"Private Roxton," said a voice behind her, deep and unhurried, "your flank is entirely exposed."

She turned too late—another snowball struck her shoulder. Captain Fielding stood at ease, a ready sphere of snow in his hand, his expression that infuriating mixture of amusement and calm.

"You might have warned me sooner!" she accused, brushing her cloak.

"I was observing your tactics. Bravery in abundance, but no cover. You will be overrun."

"Then assist me, sir, if you are so superior."

He stooped, shaped his projectile with efficient precision, and loosed it in one clean motion. It sailed straight to its mark—Roger, once again too bold—sending the boy sprawling into a drift, roaring with laughter. The children cheered their new adversary, and Merry found herself absurdly pleased, though she pretended otherwise.

"You have merely made yourself their target," she informed him.

"So be it. A soldier expects no less." He crouched to build a makeshift barrier to hide behind, eyes glinting in the winter light.

Together they held the line, side by side. Merry's laughter came fast as the cold bit at her cheeks and hair. Once, as she bent for more snow, their gloved hands brushed, and she felt, ridiculously, as if the air had warmed for that single instant.

The battle raged until stamina failed the youngest troops and peace was declared in the form of an armistice: hot milk within for all who surrendered. Flushed and tired, the children trooped back toward the house. Merry lingered, her breath clouding the air, watching the twilight gather across the white lawn.

Captain Fielding remained beside her, his coat dusted in powder. He looked not like the distant soldier of last night's dinner, but like a man entirely present—cheeks ruddy, eyes bright, his smile unguarded. "You fight well, Miss Roxton."

"You were not poor yourself, Captain. Though I do suspect you were holding back."

He gave a half-shrug, the ghost of laughter in his eyes. "I have seen enough battles. It is a pleasure to have one without casualties."

Their gazes met—just a moment too long for comfort. Merry felt her heart stir in that inconvenient way she was learning to dread. She looked away, brushing snow from her cloak. "Come, before they drink all the milk and leave us none."

They walked back together, the truce between them as fragile as the snow beneath their boots, and just as uncertain how long it would last.

CHAPTER 4

Snow had a way of softening the world, smoothing its edges until even the roughest hedgerow looked like something contrived by an ethereal hand. Joshua had marched through snow that froze a man's boots solid and buried supply wagons in drifts, but Gloucestershire snow was gentler—thin, sparkling layers that caught the moonlight and seemed to lend a hush to every sound.

It was under such a sky that the Fielding and Roxton families, wrapped in cloaks and mufflers, walked down the lane toward the church for the Christmas Eve service. Lanterns swung from poles carried by the older boys, their glow falling in golden pools upon the whitened road. Excited chatter rose and fell, and every breath made clouds of silver in the frosty air.

Joshua walked with Roger on one side, who was determined to prove he could carry his lantern higher than anyone else, and Merry on the other, her gloved hand holding her cloak closed at her throat. She had tied a fur muff about her wrist, though it dangled unused, for she insisted upon pointing things out to the children—the dark outline of an owl in the trees, the sparkle of frost on a hedge, the faint light in a cottage window.

Archie was falling behind, so he scooped him up and tossed him on to his shoulders. Soon, then, Merry found herself with little Rose on her hip.

The church bell tolled as they came into the village. Its small tower, dusted white, looked like something out of a carol itself. Candles already glimmered through the leaded glass panes, and a warm trickle of music drifted from within—bells ringing, voices laughing. Inside, the little church was bright with evergreens. Holly branches filled every nook, evergreen boughs hung over the pew ends, and a great spray of ivy curved around the pulpit. The scent was of beeswax, wood smoke, and the cold breath of many people in close quarters. Families pressed together in the narrow pews, every bonnet and coat steaming slightly as snow melted from their shoulders.

The Fielding and Roxton party filled several rows. Joshua found himself beside Merry once more—whether by accident or conspiracy of their mothers, he could not be sure. He told himself it was immaterial. She smelt faintly of cloves, no doubt from having handled the spiced cakes earlier. He tried not to notice.

The vicar, who knew better than to be too long-winded on Christmas Eve, led them through carols and prayers. Then came the moment the children had been waiting for: the Nativity.

A curtain of bedsheets had been strung across the chancel, and when it drew back, there stood the manger, constructed of rough planks, with a doll carefully swaddled in white to represent the Christ child. Behind it, a row of children in makeshift angel wings of muslin and tinsel sang a carol in voices both high and sweet.

Merry leaned forward as the little shepherds came tumbling in, wooden crooks in hand. One boy forgot his lines and announced stoutly, "We saw angels, and they were very loud," which brought muffled laughter from the pews. The angels attempted to look stern and failed.

Then came the Magi, solemn in dressing gowns borrowed from fathers, with wooden crowns painted gold. The tallest of them carried a box so heavy it nearly tipped him into the hay, and the vicar's wife had to steady him. Through it all, the doll in the manger lay serenely swaddled, as if impervious to the chaos of the world it had come to redeem.

Joshua felt something tighten in his chest as the children knelt before it, singing, 'Hark the Herald Angels Sing'. He had seen battle-fields on Christmas Eve, with men huddled round fires, singing in tongues not their own, and he thought suddenly of them—all those who had not come home to their families. He glanced at Merry. She was singing too, softly, her green eyes fixed on the little manger as though she saw more than muslin and straw.

It unsettled him that he could be moved by her quiet devotion almost as much as by the carol itself. He looked away quickly, to the frost forming patterns on the window-panes.

The service drew to a close with prayers for the King, for peace, for the harvests and hearths of the parish. Families lingered, exchanging greetings and compliments, and admiring the children's efforts. Joshua found himself engaged in conversation with an old tenant farmer, Mr. Carter, who remembered him as a lad who had once fallen through the ice on the millpond. Merry laughed when this story was retold—"I remember! He came home as soaked as a sponge, and swore me to silence lest Mrs. Fielding forbid him to go skating ever again."

It was then, just as the company was preparing to depart, that Barnaby Tremaine arrived.

The door creaked open with a gust of icy air, and heads turned. He entered not as a man hurrying from some innocent delay, but with the slow confidence of one who knows he will be noticed. His coat was of excellent cut, though dusted with snow as if he had travelled in haste. His cravat was loosened—slightly, but enough for Joshua to mark it. His eyes were too bright, his smile a shade too broad.

Merry's expression flickered. Relief, Joshua considered, for she had no doubt expected him, but there was also something else—an unease she tried at once to smother.

"Where have you been, Mr. Tremaine?" she asked lightly, as if she did not care. "You have missed the entire service."

"Business detained me," he said smoothly. "There was a gathering at Bruton's farm—cocks to be tested, wagers to be made. I could not refuse the invitation, you understand, but I would not miss the Christmas service for the world, although I see I am late."

He laughed, as though cock-fights and church services belonged to the same programme of a gentleman's amusements. The villagers nearby exchanged glances, some disapproving, some eager for gossip.

Joshua said nothing, but the words pressed against his teeth: cock-fights on Christmas Eve, and strong drink in his step. That was the man she would trust? Joshua should feel relief that Tremaine was doing the proving himself, but he did not care to see Merry hurt.

Merry attempted to smile, though it did not reach her eyes. She touched Tremaine's sleeve with a courtesy that looked rehearsed, then excused herself to help gather the younger children into their cloaks. Joshua watched her cross the little nave, head held high, and thought she carried herself in the manner of a woman who had just glimpsed a crack in a mirror she had polished too carefully.

Outside, the snow had thickened into a steady fall. Lanterns swung once more as families began the walk back up the lane. Children skipped and sang snatches of carols, while the adults discussed the Nativity with fond amusement. Merry walked ahead with the younger ones, adjusting scarves, her voice light but her expression distracted. Tremaine strode beside her, talking too loudly of wagers won and lost.

Joshua kept a little behind, silent and watchful. He told himself it was not his business. Yet the sight of Merry glancing sideways at Tremaine, her smile uncertain, lodged itself in him like a thorn.

The snow crunched beneath their boots, the bell tolled behind them, and Joshua thought grimly that this Christmas Eve had set more than one revelation alight. The parents ushered their children upstairs to bed, then returned for a while of parlour games and visiting carollers, but eventually the house settled into its Christmas Eve hush, and the great log burned with a steady glow, as if determined to keep vigil until morning.

Joshua lingered near the hearth, a glass of mulled wine cooling in his hand. He ought to have retired as well, but the weight of the evening pressed upon him—the sight of the Nativity, the memory of men who had not lived to see another Christmas, and most of all the look on Merry's face when Tremaine spoke of cock-fights as though they were not a barbaric pastime.

He was still turning over these thoughts in his mind when his mother came quietly into the room. She carried her knitting—though he doubted she could see in the dim light—and seated herself across from him with the familiarity of one who had never asked permission to share her children's confidences.

"You are restless," she observed, without preamble.

He smiled faintly. "It is the soldier's habit, perhaps."

Her needles clicked a few times before she added, "You do not like Mr. Tremaine."

Joshua drew in a breath. "Have I been so plain?"

"Not plain, only clear to a mother who has eyes." She looked at him steadily. "Is it because of what he was, or because of what he is?"

"Both," Joshua admitted. "As a boy he was arrogant, thoughtless and cruel in small ways that reveal much. As a man…tonight he walked into a church smelling of drink and boasting of wagers on cock-fights. If that is improvement, I shudder to think what decline would look like."

His mother's lips pressed together, although she did not immediately reply. At last she said, "Merry has always been dear to me, you know. I cannot pretend I am not troubled by the idea of her bound to a man whose pleasures run so shallow. Yet we cannot interfere; she must see for herself."

"What I fear," Joshua said quietly, "is that she will not see until it is too late."

Mrs. Fielding set down her needles. "Joshua, you have returned to us with scars you think hidden. You carry burdens none of us can lighten. But do not make it your burden to order another's heart. Warn her if you must. Protect her if you can. Beyond that, you must trust her judgement."

He bowed his head. She was right, and he had no claims to prevent

Miss Roxton making the mistake. Yet he could not shake the memory of Merry's uncertain smile in the candlelit nave.

"I will try," he said at last.

His mother reached across, touched his hand briefly, and then, with a softness that startled him, said, "It is not only her welfare that troubles you, is it?"

Joshua looked into the fire and did not answer.

MERRY AWOKE to the sound of bells. Not the solemn peal of church or the clamour of alarms, but the light chiming of the children who had discovered the basket of hand-bells used in the choir. They were running up and down the passage outside her chamber, jangling away with triumph, and she could not find it in her heart to scold them for Christmas had dawned, and the whole house was alive with it.

She rose quickly, for the air was sharp and the windows etched with frost. Pulling a shawl about her shoulders, she leaned over the sill. The garden below lay hushed and white, each shrub capped in snow, each branch glittering in the pale sun. Footprints marked the path where some adventurous child had already stolen out. It was a morning made for joy.

Yet Merry's thoughts did not rise with the bells. Instead they drifted back to the night before—Mr. Tremaine's late arrival, careless and a little too loud. She had told herself at the time it was nothing. Gentlemen of fashion amused themselves in many ways—cock-fights were hardly unheard of—but on Christmas Eve? And then to boast of it, when the children had only just sung of peace and goodwill?

She pressed her brow to the cold pane. His smile had been as polished as ever, but there had been something in his eyes, a brightness not entirely natural. She knew enough of men's indulgences to guess at it. A little wine might be excused, but she could not shake the image of him entering God's house with such a swagger.

Worse than her unease was the knowledge that Captain Fielding had noticed too. She had caught the flicker in his gaze, the tightening of his jaw…and though she resented his presumption, she could not deny a small, unwelcome relief that he had seen what she had seen.

She brought a pensive finger to her lip. Was the feeling more to do with the fact that she wanted to prove him wrong or that it enhanced his case?

A knock sounded, and Penelope entered, cheeks already flushed from the morning's bustle. "Merry, you must come down. The little ones are wild, and Mama insists we help keep order." Merry managed a laugh and tied her ribbons. "Very well. Give me but a moment."

When Penelope had gone, she looked once more into the snow-bright garden. She thought of Barnaby's bow, of the compliments which glided so easily from his tongue. Then she thought of Joshua—his grave steadiness, the way he had led the children's snowball fight without once making himself its hero. One dazzled; the other anchored. She ought to know which she preferred, but it was not as though the Captain was offering himself. No, he was merely trying to prove the other unworthy.

With a sigh, she drew her cloak about her and left the room. Christmas morning waited, with all its noise and laughter, but some-where beneath it all lingered a question she could not yet answer: Had she been wrong about Barnaby Tremaine? If so, then what path should she follow?

Christmas breakfast at Wychwood Hall was less a meal than a carnival. Children included in everything at Wychwood, wriggled like eels upon their benches, sneaked sugar-plums having made them excitable, and the adults bore it all with the patience of those long used to disorder. Merry sat between two of her nephews, making certain spoons remained in bowls and napkins were not flung into the fire.

But rather than gifts, the morning's pleasure was carols. After the dishes had been cleared by the servants, everyone gathered in the music-room, and Penelope took her seat at the pianoforte.

The children crowded around, holding sheets of paper they scarcely needed, for they sang more with vigour than with tune.

"I Saw Three Ships," began in respectable harmony, though Roger insisted on being the page boy with such vigour that he sang over half the others. Then came 'The Holly and the Ivy,' sweet and lilting, followed by 'God Rest Ye Merry, Gentlemen', in which the gentlemen were anything but restful, booming the chorus until the chandeliers shook.

Merry sang with the others, her voice rising more from affection than a skill she knew she did not possess. She glanced once at Captain Fielding, who did not sing loudly but carried the line firmly as one would expect from him. The children were drawn to him despite his notable lack of softness.

Archie all but climbed into his lap in order to catch the words, and shy Rose pressed close to his side. Merry could not help but notice how naturally he bore it—no show, no fuss, simply the quiet strength of a man who was obeyed.

After the carols came games. Forfeits were played with much shrieking—Penelope lost hers and was commanded to recite a verse while balancing a plum pudding upon her head, which she did with such good humour that the younger ones nearly expired from laughter. Snapdragon was attempted, raisins plucked from blue flames with shrieks of triumph and failure, though more brandy was spilled than consumed with the fruit. And through it all, Joshua Fielding was the children's unquestioned captain—directing, encouraging, never impatient.

Merry caught herself smiling too often. She reminded herself sternly that Barnaby Tremaine was equally attentive in his way.

The day brightened as the sun climbed, and soon the call went up for sledging. The snow lay crisp along the sloping meadow behind the house, untouched but for a fox's neat tracks. The older boys had already dragged out wooden sledges from the barn and polished their runners with hopeful hands.

"Come, Merry!" Roger seized her cloak. "You promised to ride with us!"

She had promised no such thing, but her protests were drowned in cheers. Archie and Edmund immediately dashed away to fetch cloaks and boots, and in a merry procession they trooped to the hill.

The first runs were chaos, with the children piling two and three upon a sledge and shrieking all the way down until they tumbled in heaps at the bottom. Joshua tested a runner, adjusted a rope, then gave Roger's sledge a proper push, sending him flying true down the hill. Cheers erupted. Soon, every child insisted upon Captain Fielding's hand at their start, declaring him luck itself.

Merry watched, laughing, as he obliged them all. He carried sledges back up when smaller arms flagged, dusted snow from flushed cheeks, and never once appeared weary of the clamour. Her heart did an odd, rebellious flutter. She remembered his words from the night before—'Soldiers do not always return'—and thought what a pity it would have been if he had not returned.

They had nearly worn themselves out with runs when another figure appeared at the edge of the meadow. Barnaby Tremaine, splendid as ever in a fur-collared coat, his boots far too fine for trudging snow, strode down as though arriving at a ball rather than a slope of noisy children.

"Miss Roxton!" he called, raising his hat. "You make the snow look pale."

The compliment, practised as it was, brought a flush to her cheeks —for she disliked having every ear within hearing of it. She managed a smile. "Mr. Tremaine, you are late to the sport."

"I should not be late at all if I had known there was sport to be had." His eyes lingered upon her face, then shifted toward Joshua, who had just launched Edmund down the hill. Something sharpened in his expression. "Ah. The soldier has turned nursemaid."

Joshua heard, for he turned, though his face betrayed no flicker of offence. "It is easier than managing recruits," he said simply, and bent to adjust another sledge.

Barnaby laughed, though it rang a little too loud. "Then let us see if soldiering teaches a man to keep pace on the hill. Shall we race, Captain?"

The children squealed at the idea, keen for a contest. Merry hesitated. Something in Barnaby's tone unsettled her, but to object would only heighten the tension. Joshua rose, snow clinging to his coat, and inclined his head. "If you wish it."

Two sledges were brought up and placed side by side. Roger was appointed starter and puffed out his chest with the importance of the role. Merry stood back with the others, her heart curiously tight.

"Ready!" Roger cried, raising his mittened hand. "Go!"

Down the hill they flew—Joshua steady, his sledge carving straight and swift. Barnaby leaned forward far too eagerly, his finer boots slipping as he pushed off. For a moment, they ran neck and neck, snow spraying in glittering arcs, but Joshua held his line while Barnaby's sledge wobbled, then struck a hidden lump and swerved. With a cry of frustration, he tumbled sideways into a drift, while Joshua flew cleanly to the bottom, snow rising in applause.

Cheers erupted from the children. Roger and Edmund whooped. Joshua rose, brushing snow from his coat, and only laughed when the boys crowded around him as though he had won a tournament.

Barnaby emerged from the drift, his cravat askew, his face dark with anger. "A child's trick hill," he muttered, too loudly. "It proves nothing."

"Oh, but it proves everything!" Roger declared with wicked delight. "Uncle Joshua won fair, and you fell!"

Barnaby's eyes flashed; for an instant, Merry feared he might scold the boy. Instead he forced a laugh that was strained and thin. "Well, perhaps the soldier can manage toys, after all."

The words fell flat. The children frowned and looked away, and Merry felt a hot flush rise to her cheeks—not of pleasure, but of shame for him. A gentleman should lose a race with grace; Barnaby had lost with petulance.

Joshua merely lifted Roger onto his shoulders and said mildly, "The hill has chosen its champion." The children roared approval, and Barnaby's laugh grew harsher.

"A childish remark, as one might expect."

He held out his arm to Merry and they followed along behind the crowd of children clamouring about Captain Fielding on the return to the house.

CHAPTER 5

*J*oshua watched the flicker of disappointment cross Merry's face. Barnaby Tremaine, brushing at his fur collar with impatient fingers and laughing too loudly at his own misfortune, looked every inch the spoiled child denied a treat. It had been a simple race, yet Tremaine must turn an honest tumble into insult. The children's cheers for Joshua had not been gloating. They were the uncomplicated joy of small creatures who love a sure line and a true finish. But Tremaine perceived mockery where there was none and answered it with a sneer thin enough to show the grain beneath the polish.

Joshua felt something within himself loosen by a degree. He had planned to observe, inquire, and gather proofs and present them to Merry. This afternoon taught him he need not. Tremaine was conducting his own campaign of ruin. The question that lodged in Joshua's mind was not whether Tremaine would unmask himself, but whether Merry would accept a mask she knew to be false for the petty respectability of a title and a carriage crest.

He did not think her mercenary. She had never looked so little like a girl who counted vanities as when she had knelt to tie a child's boot-lace on the icy hill, but he knew, better than most, how years of being told one is almost good enough can wear grooves into judgement. A cit's daughter courted by a baron's son received more counsel than she bargained for.

His brooding lasted only as long as the boys allowed. Roger discovered that his hero could be made to shoulder a sledge and three children at once. Edmund declared that any gentleman who had won a race must necessarily toss each of his admirers into a bank of snow in celebration, followed by a chorus of voices: "Me first, Uncle Joshua! Me first!" The honour of man did not, at present, require a philosophical answer about Merry's marriage. It required a man with strong arms and a willingness to be used.

"Very well," he said, suppressing a laugh, "but you will mind the rules: one at a time, no ambuscades, and no tears when you are buried as deep as Buonaparte's hopes."

"Will there be drums?" Archie demanded, already scrambling into Joshua's hold.

"There will be a drum made of your belly when you land," Joshua returned, and with a swift pivot, he tossed the boy into a drift so soft and powdery that he went in with a whoop and emerged a moment later, snow-covered and triumphant.

"I want a go too!" cried Rose, too small for hurling but eager for some share of the ritual.

"For you," Joshua said, hoisting her gently and setting her into a miniature puddle of snow as if she were the queen of a frosted island. She crowed and clapped mittened hands.

One by one he fulfilled the absurd ceremony—Roger, Edmund, Archie, Rose, and Jasper, the youngest, who, after much persuasion, consented to a very shallow drift and came up laughing with a face like a sugared bun.

It was then that Tremaine let slip a remark pitched to travel—one of those silken sentences meant to be overheard and to bite. "I see the Captain has found his proper station," he said to no one in particular, and yet to everyone. "It is a comfort when men discover their talents lie in the nursery rather than in company."

Joshua's back had taken worse from a French sabre than from a gentleman's insinuation, and he had no particular itch to answer. He set Rose down, adjusted her muffler, and said only, "One must rise to one's level, Mr. Tremaine. I am just tall enough to catch children when they fall."

There was a small sound—Merry's breath, half-laugh, half-warning. Tremaine coloured, not with shame but with resentment at having been denied his provocation. "Come, Miss Roxton," he said, offering an arm to escort her back toward the house as if he had cleared the way for her. "You cannot prefer the wind to the fire."

Merry hesitated—Joshua saw it, though it lasted no longer than a snowflake on a glove—and then, in the habit of a young lady trained to spare others embarrassment, she took the arm. He spoke to her as one would speak to a person halfway decided upon, with an undertone Joshua recognized as ownership rehearsed to appear as courtesy.

Joshua gathered the sledges and the smaller troops and headed back.

By the time they reached the wide steps of Wychwood, all cheeks were apple-bright and all gloves ingloriously wet. The door opened to a rush of warm air and the welcome scent of wood smoke and cloves. Servants descended to take cloaks, and mothers applied that peculiar maternal inspection which scolds whilst hovering.

"Warm milk for the regiment," Mr. Roxton declared, and Joshua wondered to himself if they always made so many army references, or were only doing so to humour him.

He allowed himself to be shepherded towards the great hearth, where the yule log radiated comfort from its red heart. The children installed themselves upon the rug, milk and slices of seed cake having been distributed to all.

Tremaine took up a position with studied negligence upon the far side of the hearth, Merry beside him in a chair before the fire. Joshua, who had determined to cease such convoluted thinking for at least ten minutes, found thought settling to him as snow settles on a hedge. He had told himself he could be content to remain unmarried—that the army required a man's whole self, and that any other pretence was unfair to the woman persuaded to accept half. He had believed it too, in the dogged way a soldier believes the weather is what it is. Yet the last twenty-four hours had worked upon that certainty. There had been the children's adoration—artless, unbought. There had been Merry's laughter, not at him but with him. There had been an odd sensation on the hill when a little hand had slipped into his and trusted, without argument, that he would set the owner of it down safe. He had always supposed such things belonged to other men— men who did not sleep with their boots ready by the bed. It came to him, disconcertingly, that he wanted them—not in a vague someday, not as a sop to the decorum of his elders, but as a thing he would miss if he allowed it to pass—a wife, children, noise, warmth, a home that was not transient. The army was woven into him, but he was not dependent upon it. He had set out to prove himself capable of making his own way, and now he had nothing left to prove. Besides, most of their work was now situated in and about London.

He became aware he was staring at Merry. Tremaine, animated by the prospect of an audience unwilling or unable to flee, was recounting some anecdote from the cock-fight the previous day, adjusting it to be nearly respectable, and was working at the impossible arithmetic of making brutality sound like taste. Merry's smile was courteous and cool. When Tremaine said, "Of course, a gentleman must keep up appearances. One cannot live altogether by country rules," there was an emphasis upon gentleman that shaved the word like a blade. And when he turned to Merry with, "You will find, too, the mistress of a great house cannot always do as she likes," the warning sang through the sentence like a note below the melody. "You will have nurses and nursemaids to help."

Merry blushed.

Joshua's fingers clenched and released against the curve of his mug. He had no right—and yet he felt it as a man feels a brand to the skin.

MERRY REFUSED TO FEEL BELITTLED. Whatever small sting his tone carried, he could not mean it. Barnaby Tremaine was simply careless, too used to his own way to mind how his words landed. He did not even realize how a look might sometimes cut like a blade. It was only the manner of a man who had always been obeyed and admired. He could not help it. That was what she told herself. She made excuse after excuse, as though each one might shield her pride. He meant nothing by it. He did not know how it sounded. He did not mean to belittle.

Her pride did not soften when he reached into his pocket and produced a small velvet case. He offered it with a flourish, bowing so low that several cousins turned their heads to watch.

"A token of the season," he said.

Inside lay a bracelet of worked gold, the kind of ornament a lady might wear in London with perfect consequence. Small stones glittered in the firelight, so fine and numerous they seemed far above the simple attentions of courtship. Merry's breath caught in her throat. Such a gift was not offered lightly. Surely this meant more? Surely it was the first step toward a declaration?

She lifted her eyes, but Tremaine only smiled, watching her delight as if it were amusement to him. He said nothing more. He seemed content that she should gape at the splendour.

"It is beautiful," she said, her voice steady though her thoughts tumbled, "but I cannot accept it."

His brows rose. "Why not?"

"Because we are not betrothed. It would not be proper."

"What, that?" He laughed and waved his hand as if she had mistaken a diamond for a daisy. "It is a trifle. Nothing more. Do not make it heavier than it is. Wear it, Merry. It becomes you."

She let him fasten the clasp, although unease pricked at her like hidden thorns. The gold lay cool and heavy on her wrist. He admired it, his gaze fixed more on the bracelet than on her face, and she wondered if the gift were meant to adorn her or to display his own generosity.

Still, she excused him. Perhaps he thought the gift would please her family, a sign of his serious intentions. Perhaps he meant to speak later. Perhaps his silence was only hesitation. Surely he could not trifle with her so publicly?

After a little while, he asked her to walk him out. He must leave soon for dinner with his family, but he wished for a word first. She followed him into the hall, her pulse quick with expectation. This must be it. He would speak now.

The hall was hushed, hung with ivy and holly, the great ball of mistletoe swaying from its ribbon above them. Tremaine looked up at it and then down at her, his smile too knowing.

"You know the custom," he said.

Her heart sank. "Is that all you brought me here to say?"

"Why not? A kiss beneath the mistletoe, and we might call it a *merry* Christmas indeed." He chuckled.

She stood her ground. "You have never introduced me to your family. Not once have you invited me into their company. Why is that?"

He blinked, then recovered. "The occasion has not arisen. My father is busy with matters of estate. My mother is delicate. They are not in sufficient health for company."

"You have been in the neighbourhood for weeks," she pressed. "If you intended me to be a part of your future, would you not wish me to know those who will also be mine?"

He shifted uneasily. "There will be time for that. Why press them now? Families are often cautious, and it is best to wait until all is secure. You must trust me."

The words poured smoothly, yet none of them satisfied. She felt the weight of the bracelet as if it were a shackle. She had asked for clarity and been given evasions. She had hoped for tenderness and been met with talk of caution.

"So this bracelet is nothing more than a trifle?" she asked.

He laughed, careless once more. "Of course. Why weigh it with meaning? It is a gift, nothing more. Wear it and think no further."

He leaned toward her, his eyes glinting. "Come, Merry. Give me a kiss under the mistletoe, and let us end the day pleasantly."

Before she could protest, his lips brushed hers. She had imagined such a moment more times than she would ever admit, had thought it must feel like magic when it came at last. Instead there was nothing—no spark, no sweetness—only the pressure of lips that seemed to demand rather than cherish. He tried to deepen the kiss, drawing closer, his hand tightening at her waist as if determined to claim more than she wished to give.

Merry stiffened. Disappointment swelled into alarm. She pushed against his chest, breaking free, her breath quick and sharp. "No, Mr. Tremaine. Not unless you are prepared to speak plainly."

He laughed, though the sound rang hollow. "You are spirited, Merry. That is part of your charm."

But she did not laugh. The kiss had left her cold. It had been nothing like the joy she had hoped, and everything like the hollow gift glittering on her wrist.

His smile faltered, then slid back into place. "Another time, then. My father waits, and I must be gone. Think kindly of me while I am absent."

He bowed and left her beneath the mistletoe, his boots sharp against the stone.

When the door closed, the sprig swayed gently in the draught. Merry stood motionless. She unclasped the bracelet and turned it over in her hands. It glittered in the light, but it felt cold, false, a promise that meant nothing. She slipped it back into its case.

Her mind leaped between excuses and doubts. Perhaps he was shy of declaring before his parents. Perhaps he feared his father's disapproval. Perhaps he wished to be certain of her answer before involving his family. She tried to believe it. Yet the memory of his smooth evasions, his eagerness for a kiss when he had given her no true claim upon him, refused to be silenced.

She thought of Captain Fielding. Never would he have pressed her with laughter and half-answers. Never would he have called such a gift a trifle. His bluntness might wound her pride, but at least she always knew where she stood with him. There was a steadiness in him, a weight of truth that asked no adornment. He might not think to bring a bracelet sparkling with stones, but if ever he placed anything in her hands, she believed it would be something she could trust.

The fire in the hall crackled, the voices of her family rose from the parlour, but Merry felt apart from it all. The glittering bracelet lay in its case in her pocket, and she thought how easily glitter might dazzle the eye while leaving the heart unsatisfied.

She closed the case and carried it upstairs. She could not yet say what her heart had decided, but she knew one thing with certainty. This gift did not feel like joy.

CHAPTER 6

The snow fell thickly that Christmas night, yet the village was lively all the same. Joshua had thought to pass the evening quietly at Wychwood, but his brothers insisted upon a walk down to the Green. They claimed it was to see the lanterns and join the carols that would be sung outside the tavern, though Joshua suspected more curiosity than devotion drew them forth. He had not walked abroad with them in years and found the prospect oddly warming, so he joined the party, pulling his greatcoat tightly to him against the cold.

The village glowed with merriment. Candles shone in windows, evergreen boughs hung over doors, and laughter rose from within the Shaven Crown where most of the village's men had gathered, the large wooden beams angled to a high point and a roaring fire at the end welcoming them. Joshua's brothers soon melted into the throng, greeting neighbours with loud good cheer, while Joshua lingered at the edge, content to observe.

It was then he noticed Tremaine. The man had not joined them at church earlier, nor remained long at Wychwood after his ill-timed gift to Merry. Yet here he was now, at a table in the corner of the tavern, the light of several candles casting a golden haze about his handsome features. Cards lay in his hands, a pile of coin and notes already scattered before him. A painted wench perched upon his lap, laughing too freely, her bodice cut lower than was decent. Tremaine seemed in high spirits, wagering with reckless abandon, his voice carrying above the din.

Joshua moved nearer, unnoticed in the crush of bodies. He had spent too many years learning how to watch without being watched to forget the habit. What he heard troubled him. Tremaine cursed his luck one moment and boasted of his winnings the next.

Joshua lingered near the doorway, the cold air rushing in each time a new patron entered, and watched the game unfold. Tremaine's table grew louder as the night lengthened. The painted woman in his lap leaned across him, her laughter shrill and grating, while the men at his side grew increasingly unruly with every round of cards.

Joshua recognized one of them now—a stocky fellow with a scar over his brow, known as Jem Kettle, a man once hauled before the courts for cheating dice but acquitted for lack of proof. The other was a lean squire with the kind of pallor that comes from too many nights spent in smoke-filled rooms. Neither man bore the respectability of good company, yet Tremaine greeted them as familiars.

At first, Tremaine played with easy confidence. He tossed coins onto the table with a flourish, laughing when he won, laughing louder when he lost. The wench kissed his cheek when his hand triumphed and pouted prettily when it did not. However, as the pile before the man dwindled, Joshua saw his smile grow tighter. He drank more quickly, called for another bottle, and leaned forward with a glare that did not match the careless flick of his cards.

"Another fifty," Tremaine said, his voice raised above the din.

Jem Kettle grinned, showing a row of yellowed teeth. "Done, my lord. But mind you can pay when the reckoning comes."

The squire chuckled. "He has ways. Do not fear for Barnaby Tremaine."

Tremaine's colour rose. "I have never failed to pay a debt in my life."

The scarred man winked. "Then your pa must have deep pockets."

The next hand was dealt. Tremaine's fingers drummed against the wood while he studied his cards. The wench leaned across him again, whispering advice in his ear, though her eyes flicked toward the largest stack of coins on the table. Tremaine pushed her aside with an irritated jerk of his shoulder, earning a pout and a muttered curse.

When the cards were shown, his hand failed again. The laughter of his companions rang out, harsh and cruel.

"Hard luck, Tremaine," the squire said, gathering in the notes with long, pale fingers. "It seems fortune does not favour you tonight."

Tremaine's jaw clenched. "Deal again."

The wench tried to soothe him, trailing her fingers along his collar, but he struck her hand away. The gesture was small, yet ugly. His voice grew louder and sharper, as though volume could disguise desperation.

Joshua watched with steady eyes. This was no picture of a gentleman at harmless play. It was the portrait of a man bleeding coin he could not afford, snarling when the mask of polish slipped. His losses grew deep, and his temper deeper still. And Merry—bright, trusting Merry—thought to bind herself to this man—to share in his ruin.

Joshua's resolve hardened like frost. He could not allow Merry to walk blindly into such a snare.

He stepped back, unsettled by what he had seen. The picture told itself plainly enough. Tremaine was a man living beyond his means, seeking his salvation in cards and wagers—and when the stakes failed him, he would turn elsewhere. To Merry.

It was then that a rough hand touched Joshua's sleeve. He turned and saw Will Fletcher, an old seaman who had once sailed with his father's ships and now worked as a steward for them. Fletcher had a face lined like a chart and eyes that missed little.

"Captain Fielding," the man said quietly. "A word, if you will grant it."

Joshua followed him out into the cold, where the snow muffled their voices. Fletcher glanced about to be certain no-one lingered nearby.

"I thought you should know, sir," he began, "there is talk in London of Mr. Tremaine meeting with men of ill repute. Investors, they call themselves, but they are more rogues than merchants. I have seen the sort before, the kind that promise fortunes and deliver ruin. They have had their claws in several young gentlemen this past year."

Joshua's mouth tightened. "And you are certain Tremaine was among them?"

"I saw him with my own eyes not three months past, in company with a fellow named Carter who lost a ship in dock through fraud and near cost your father dear. They met in a coffee-house near the Exchange, whispering like two smugglers over a bargain. I marked it, for Mr. Tremaine is not the sort I should expect to see in such company."

Joshua drew in a breath, the cold air burning his lungs. The pieces began to arrange themselves. Tremaine's reckless gaming, his eagerness to dazzle, his sudden attentions to Merry—these were not the pursuits of a man courting for affection. They were the strategies of a desperate gambler seeking to mend his fortunes by other means.

"You have my thanks, Fletcher," Joshua said. "You have done me a service."

The old seaman tipped his hat. "I thought it right you should know. Miss Roxton deserves better."

So Fletcher knew of Merry's hopes in that regard, Joshua mused. It would not be long before the entire village knew of Tremaine's losses, and then surely would its inhabitants speculate about his intentions towards her.

Joshua returned to the tavern only long enough to collect his brothers and steer them homeward. They grumbled good-naturedly at being torn from the merriment, but Joshua had no patience left for their jests. His mind was already turning to what must be done.

Back at Wychwood, he retired early to his chamber and lit a single candle upon the desk. The house lay quiet, the muffled sound of distant carols drifting through the frosted glass. He drew out paper and pen, the familiar ritual steadying his thoughts.

·   ·   ·

To Colonel Renforth, Harcourt House, London.

He wrote swiftly, the words of a soldier accustomed to reports, though he softened them for a friend.

Sir,

You will forgive me for troubling you in the midst of the festive season, yet I have need of your discretion. A certain gentleman of Gloucestershire, Mr. Barnaby Tremaine, son of Lord Bruton, has lately made himself a constant visitor among my family's circle. His conduct here has raised questions, and I have reason to suspect his circumstances are not what they appear. Rumours speak of gaming debts and disreputable acquaintances in London. I beg you to make discreet inquiries among our mutual friends in Town, especially those with knowledge of the gaming houses and the Exchange. I do not ask for scandal, only for truth. If there is nothing in it, I shall be glad. If there is, I must know before harm is done to someone I hold dear.

I remain your respectful and obedient servant,
  Fielding

He sanded the page, folded and sealed it, and addressed it for the morning post.

When it was done, he sat back, the quill still in his fingers. The work was familiar. In Spain and Portugal he had been tasked with uncovering enemy movements, nosing out spies, and protecting his men from betrayal. Now there was peace, he still worked in a secret capacity, finding himself using the same skills at home—watching, listening, piecing together whispers. The battlefield had changed, but the duty had not.

Joshua stared into the candle flame, his thoughts returning to Merry. He saw her as she had been that afternoon, snow caught in her hair, laughter bright upon her lips, the children clinging to her skirts as if she were their general. She deserved a man who cherished her, not one who sought her fortune.

He clenched his hand until the quill snapped between his fingers. No matter how carefully Tremaine concealed it, Joshua would uncover the truth...and when he did, Merry would be armed with more than rumours. She would have proof.

So much, he reflected wryly, for letting Tremaine bury himself, but matters had changed with the revelations of that night.

He blew out the candle and let the darkness close about him, the letter sealed upon the desk, his resolve to provide facts firm.

BOXING DAY dawned crisp and bright, the air keen with frost, though the sun spilled over the snow with a brilliance that made the whole countryside sparkle as if set with jewels. Merry had always loved the morning after Christmas. It lacked the grandeur of the day itself, but there was a pleasant bustle in the household. Boxes of gifts had been prepared for the servants—lengths of cloth, ribbons, stockings, spices, and purses of coin for those in long service. The family assembled in the great hall to hand them out, the children skipping about with far more noise than dignity, eager to see the grooms and maids unwrap their parcels.

Merry watched with fondness as Mrs. Fielding pressed a box into the butler's hands and thanked him for another year of diligence, while the older children ran to present baskets of fruit to the kitchen girls. The cook was nearly in tears when Roger shyly handed her a shawl he had chosen himself. There was laughter, bows, curtsies, and many grateful smiles, and Merry thought how fitting it was that those who worked so hard behind the scenes should have their own day of honour.

By mid morning, the servants had been released to enjoy their holiday, and the grand kitchen, usually a flurry of pots and pans, grew suddenly quiet. It fell to the ladies of the house to contrive a light luncheon for the family, though in truth there were so many of them that even a 'light' meal looked like a banquet. Cold meats, pickled salmon, loaves of bread, cheese, and pies were assembled on platters, with cider and ale set out for good measure.

The kitchen bustled with feminine chatter as the ladies worked side by side. Mrs. Roxton, sturdy and capable, directed the arrangement of dishes with her usual authority, while Mrs. Fielding occupied herself with trimming a plate of cakes. Penelope sliced bread with brisk efficiency, her cheeks flushed, while the Fielding brothers' wives —five of them—arranged salads and fruits.

Merry carried a plate of pigeon pies to the table, trying to look as composed as the others, though her thoughts strayed toward Barnaby Tremaine. The bracelet still lay upstairs in its box, hidden from sight but not from her mind.

"Penelope," Mrs. Roxton said, wagging a finger as her daughter reached for another knife. "Do be careful. You are as quick with your hands as your tongue, and both will land you in trouble if you do not slow down."

"I would rather be quick than dull," Penelope returned, her eyes sparkling, "and I have something worth the telling."

Her tone caught the attention of all at once. Even Mrs. Fielding looked up from her cakes.

"What is it now?" asked one of the sisters-in-law, adjusting her cap.

"My husband came home very late last night," Penelope said, lowering her voice in a way that made everyone lean closer. "As did all of the gentlemen."

The women grumbled their acknowledgement.

"They had been at the tavern, and you will not believe what he saw —or perhaps you will, if you have eyes."

Merry's heart gave an uneasy throb. She already suspected which name would follow.

"Mr. Tremaine," Penelope announced with relish, "losing heavily at cards, behaving as if money grows on trees and—most shamefully—

with a woman in his lap. And she was not a lady, if you take my meaning."

The room went very still.

"Penelope!" Mrs. Roxton exclaimed, scandalized. "There are children present, and Merry—"

"Merry is near one-and-twenty," Penelope cut in firmly. "She is old enough to hear it. It is better she should hear the truth now than be dazzled by pretty speeches later if he means to court her."

Mrs. Fielding set down her knife. "You are certain?"

"Lennox could hardly mistake it. Ask the others," Penelope said. "The fellow was drunk with losses. He threw good money after bad, swore like a sailor, and laughed as though it were all sport. And when the cards turned against him again, he kissed the woman as if that would bring him luck. Disgraceful."

The sisters-in-law murmured among themselves, their eyes darting toward Merry with thinly veiled curiosity.

Merry's face burned. She wanted to vanish into the floor. The thought of Barnaby in such company, behaving so recklessly, humiliated her to the very bone. Had she not been wearing his bracelet only yesterday? Had she not endured his kiss beneath the mistletoe, convincing herself it meant something? To hear now that he squandered coin in public and allowed such women to sit upon his knee—it made her feel foolish and naïve, even ridiculous.

Mrs. Roxton cleared her throat. "Well, if Merry wishes to marry into a higher station, she must be willing to look the other way. That is how things stand among the aristocracy. Husbands stray; wives endure. It is not admirable, but it is the way of the world."

The sisters-in-law nodded with resignation.

"It is not always so," Mrs. Fielding said quietly. "There are marriages of respect as well as convenience. Do not tar all unions with the same brush."

"Respect is well enough in stories," Mrs. Roxton countered, "but in reality most ladies must accept what they are given. If they wish for a title, they must bear the burdens of it."

"And the burdens are heavier than the jewels," one of the wives said with a sigh. "My cousin married a lord and spends half her time alone while he roves from town to town. She has gowns and a carriage but no peace."

The talk grew animated, each woman offering her own tale of some lord or baronet who kept mistresses, who squandered fortunes, who treated wives as little more than ornaments. Penelope declared she would never trade her steady husband for the grandest title in England, and Mrs. Fielding agreed, saying she valued kindness above consequence. Mrs. Roxton retorted that such talk was well enough for women who already had husbands, but a girl of one-and-twenty must think of her future.

Merry stood very still, her hands gripping the edge of the table until her knuckles whitened. The words cut deeply, each one pricking like a thorn. She had dreamed of rising above the narrow life of the Cotswolds, of stepping into something finer. And now she was told that to marry into such a world, she must accept betrayal, humiliation, and neglect as part of the bargain.

Her stomach churned. She thought of Barnaby's careless kiss, of his evasions, of the weight of the bracelet on her wrist. She thought of his easy laughter at the tavern, a woman in his lap while he lost his father's coin. Was this truly the life she wanted? To look away while her husband gambled and strayed, while she smiled through the shame?

She longed to defend herself, to protest that Barnaby was different, that he would change, but the words stuck in her throat. She no longer believed them.

Humiliation pressed down like a heavy cloak. She kept her chin high, but inside she felt small, foolish, and raw. What was she to do?

The women carried on their chatter, arranging plates and trimming pies, but Merry heard only the pounding of her own heart. She wished suddenly, fiercely, that she were back in her childhood, when all she had to fear was being scolded for climbing a tree or throwing a snowball at Joshua Fielding. Life had seemed so much simpler then… and now she did not know which way to turn.

Merry slipped away after the meal was cleared, claiming she

wished for air. No one stopped her. She wrapped her cloak close and stepped into the cold. The park stretched white and silent, the snow crisp beneath her boots, the bare trees etched against a pewter sky.

She walked without aim at first, only glad to be away from curious eyes and sharp tongues. The stillness of the park steadied her. Yet the words spoken would not leave her: 'If she wants to marry into a higher station, she must be willing to look the other way.'

Was that truly the choice? To be a lady, but receive no respect? To smile in company while her husband laughed elsewhere with women who were not her? Could she endure that humiliation? Her pride recoiled, but another voice whispered of what she might gain. She would no longer be the cit's daughter who had never been to London. She would sit at the head of a table in a great house. She would be secure, respectable, a mother.

She paused beneath an oak, the branches of which held pockets of snow, and considered the other path. To refuse Barnaby was to risk spinsterhood. What then? She would remain in the Cotswolds, unmarried, dependent upon her family's kindness. She would be 'poor Merry' to the neighbours, pitied in whispers. She would watch her sisters' children grow, and smile as though it were enough.

Would it be enough?

She drew her cloak tighter and walked on. To marry without love was bitter, but to have no marriage at all seemed colder still. There was safety in a husband's name, however careless. There was honour in being wife to a man of rank. Was not that what every girl was taught to want?

Yet her heart rebelled. She thought of that kiss under the mistletoe. It had promised nothing. It had felt like nothing. How could she bind herself to a man who stirred no spark in her, whose gaze sought jewels more than her face, whose laughter was loudest in gaming rooms? Would he grow worse in time and shame their children? Lose her fortune?

The snow crunched softly as she walked, the silence around her broken only by the distant cry of a rook. She weighed one life against another and found no comfort in either scale.

A spinster's life meant loneliness, yet it meant freedom. No husband to shame her, no vows twisted into mockery. She might never be envied, but neither would she be despised.

A marriage of convenience meant security, yet it also seemed to mean betrayal.

Merry stopped at the edge of the frozen pond and stared at her blurred reflection in the ice. "Which is worse?" she whispered. "To be alone, or to be bound to a man who does not care?"

The reflection offered no answer.

Merry turned back toward the house, her steps heavy. She had always thought herself to be practical, ready to face the world as it was, but now that the choice lay before her, she found no certainty at all.

CHAPTER 7

*J*oshua had come to know two kinds of quiet. The first was the uneasy hush that fell before a volley, when men held their breath and horses rolled their eyes at dangers still hidden. The second was the honest stillness of a winter morning in the country, when frost had laid its fine hand over every hedge and the air tasted of ice and wood smoke. He had known far too much of the former. The latter he found at Wychwood, and he craved it.

He rose before the household had shaken off its slumber. In his chamber, the embers still glowed faintly in the grate, but the air was sharp and bracing. He dressed swiftly, carried his boots in his hand to spare the corridor any noise, and descended the stair. The hall smelled of evergreen and spice, still lingering from the day before. Outside, the park gleamed, a skin of white stretched unbroken across the lawn.

Joshua had meant to exercise Brutus, his black gelding. The horse had aged as he had, though his steady temper pleased him better than youthful exuberance ever had. Yet when he reached the stable-yard, he found he was not the first to rise.

Merry stood beside a bay mare with a star upon her brow, testing the girth with quick, capable hands. Her cloak was thrown back, her hair tucked beneath a modest felt hat, and her cheeks bore the colour of the morning cold. She looked up at him, as though she had guessed it would be he who intruded, and had not quite decided whether or not to be pleased.

"Miss Roxton," Joshua greeted her, bowing with old habit even at a stable door. "You will rob the sun of his earliest glory."

"That would be a crime in Gloucestershire," she returned with a smile. "He has so few glories in December, one ought to leave him the ones he can contrive."

"Where are you off to so early?"

"To Roxton House. We have ewes lambing in the fold below the north copse, and I would see how they fare."

"Do you not have a shepherd to tend to such matters?"

"Of course," she said, fastening the strap another notch, "but I would not have my own peace of mind if I did not go."

Brutus was brought forward, tossing his head as though he, too, relished the frosty air. The groom grinned. "He'll be away like a thought if you let him, Captain."

"I shall not let him," Joshua answered, patting the strong black neck. He knew Brutus would go nowhere without him.

Merry observed him, her mare shifting beneath her. "Older, and yet improved—at least in the horse."

Smiling, Joshua mounted. "I might contest the comparison. If you do not object, I shall ride with you. It would be a pity to waste all this frost for want of conversation worthy of it."

She lifted a careless shoulder, though a spark of mischief lingered in her expression. "Very well. Only promise you will not tell me how to manage my ewes."

"I shall not presume to instruct you in sheep. My experience extends beyond horses only to mules, which hate me, and men who behave the same."

"Somehow I doubt that."

They set out down the lane, the horses' hooves cutting crescents in the frost. The air turned their breath to clouds, and the hedges glistened as though dressed in lace.

"You go often, then?" Joshua asked.

"Every day now," she replied. "Lambs do not read calendars."

"And your shepherd?"

"Old Dawkins has eyes like a hawk and hands like bark. He misses nothing…but he never minds if I ask foolish questions and pretend to be useful."

Joshua studied her as she spoke, the ease with which she described her part in the work. "I doubt the pretence. You are not half so ornamental as you would have the world believe."

"That is an insult if ever I heard one."

"It is praise in disguise. You are very bad at being merely pretty."

"You do not improve the matter, Captain," she said, though her lips curved despite her rebuke.

They reached the fold, where Old Dawkins greeted Merry with respect, Joshua noted keenly. She went among the ewes without fuss, crouching to take a shivering lamb into her arms and murmur comfort until both ewe and lamb settled. Dawkins, leaning on his stick, nodded toward her.

"She has a way," he told Joshua. "Some frighten beasts by trying to be kind. She comes, and they sense she means no harm. Born with it, she was. Miss Merry has saved more lambs than I can count, only for want of affection."

Joshua watched Merry, her auburn head bent over the lamb, and could not dispute him. "That is a gift," he said quietly.

They lingered awhile, aiding here and there. When Dawkins withdrew, Merry blew on her hands. "The sheep never ask when I mean to wed, or whether the vicar will allow the waltz," she said.

"They only require you to be faithful," Joshua returned.

Her expression wavered, and for a moment the lightness slipped. Beneath her teasing, he sensed a quiet restlessness, as if she were weighing matters not yet spoken. She rode with her chin lifted, but her eyes held the look of someone searching for answers, uncertain of what she hoped to see.

Joshua did not press her, though he felt the urge. It was in her nature to decide quickly, with the courage of a woman who preferred action to waiting. Yet he could not help but fear she might leap over a hedge when the gate was just ahead.

They turned their horses homeward, the sun higher now, the frost sparkling brighter. The church bells rang faintly across the fields, calling them back to Christmas-tide noise and family. Joshua glanced at Merry, the restlessness still lingering beneath her composure, and thought to himself that he must tread carefully. If she hurried into a future she did not deserve, it would not be because he had failed her.

THEY TOOK the longer way back to Wychwood, down a track that curved by a stand of birches and then ran straight across open meadow. The sun had climbed a little and turned the snow to a dazzle. Merry allowed her mare to break into an easy trot, and Brutus answered with a spring of eagerness. It was impossible not to admire the way man and horse moved as one.

"I am told," Merry said, fixing her eyes on the path ahead, "that in London mornings are different from these. One may sleep through them and nobody minds."

"In London, for most morning begins after noon," Joshua drawled.

She laughed. "You disdain it?"

"I am remarking upon it for people who like lamps more than sunlight—people who stay out until dawn." He looked across at her. "You would like parts of it very much. You would scorn parts of it."

"What parts would I scorn?"

"The parts that pretend crowds are an ideal to be attained. The parts that mistake glamour for goodness. Yet you would love your first sight of the theatre. You would forgive London anything for an evening at Covent Garden with a singer who can turn silence into music. You would love the bookshops and the picture galleries. I suspect you would like the Thames when it freezes and everyone pretends they can skate."

"I should like the skating," she said at once. "I should not like the noise."

"London has its virtues, but will never compete with the country for quiet."

They slowed at a gate where the hasp stuck. Joshua swung down and set it right with a firm lift. When they moved on, she said, "Would you enjoy more time in Town, Captain?"

"I enjoy London well enough when there is a reason to be there," he answered. "I like the stimulation of my work, and the company of my colleagues, who excel at it."

"Then the country suits you better, yet you would not leave the army," she said, not as a challenge, only as a fact she wished to lay beside the others.

"No," he answered. "I know the feel of that work. It is not gentle and it is not always fair, but it is rewarding. I also know that men must have more than idleness if they mean to grow old without becoming soft."

They rode on in companionable quiet. A crow lifted from the hedgerow and scolded them. Far off, the river lay like a strip of pewter, edged with ice that would harden by nightfall. She had enjoyed mornings alone all her life, although she had longed for the better pleasure of someone beside her.

"Would you live more in the country if you could?" she asked, as if she had only just given herself leave to wonder.

"Yes," he said, and the ease of the answer surprised her.

"Would you miss London?"

"Not much," he replied, and she smiled.

The path narrowed where two old oaks leaned together across it. Simultaneously, they ducked their heads through the twined branches. Merry's hat brushed a snow-laden twig and sent a soft drift over her cloak. She shook it off, laughing. Some lightness had crept back into her courtesy of his company, yet the restlessness remained.

They reached the stile where the meadow fell away toward the lower spinney. The air smelled faintly of wood smoke from a cottage beyond the ridge.

"A person could make a life of mornings like this," she said, meaning it and almost wishing she did not.

"A person could," he said, "and some would call it a small life because it looks small from a distance. On closer inspection it is a great one."

She looked aside at him. "You speak as if you had measured both."

"From too many people have I stood far-off and judged them wrongly," he said. "I hope I am learning to stand closer."

"You are quite philosophical. I would not have supposed it about you."

She felt almost content. Then she remembered the bracelet hidden away upstairs and the way Mr. Tremaine's mouth had hardened when she refused him liberties under the mistletoe. The contentment faltered, as thin as ice above a brook.

"Captain," she said, and then did not know how to shape the rest, so she said, "Thank you for the ride this morning." Then, before she could school the words, she added, "Commonly I ride alone, but I enjoyed having your company.". Heat rose in her face and somehow she turned it into a laugh. "The sheep prefer two fools to one sage," she said quickly, lest he think she was flirting with him. She must remember her purpose.

They topped the last rise. Wychwood lay below them, calm beneath its winter cap. The roofs and chimneys were softened by snow. Merry's spirits had lifted, too—her cheeks still tingled from the cold air, her heart quickened with the glad sense of being alive, of sharing a morning that had felt unusually free.

As they began their descent, she thought how very nearly perfect it had all been. The crisp air, the steady mare beneath her, the companionable quiet with Joshua. At that moment, she might have believed that life could be simple.

The road curved past the gates of Lord Bruton's manor, tall and imposing even beneath its frosting of snow. Merry glanced through them idly, expecting only to see the wide sweep of lawn, the dark evergreens edging the drive. What she did see struck her like a slap.

Across the lawn, cutting twin tracks in the snow, sped a shining sleigh. The horse's bells jingled gaily, and Barnaby Tremaine himself held the reins, handsome in his dark coat, his posture the very picture of ease. Beside him sat a lady wrapped in fur, her bonnet trimmed with crimson ribbons. She leaned close, laughing as though the world held no shadows, her face lifted to Barnaby's with unguarded delight.

Merry's breath caught. She stiffened in the saddle.

Joshua saw it too—she felt rather than witnessed the change in him, the way his horse shifted in response to his hand. But he said nothing. He did not need to. The sight spoke loudly enough.

Barnaby had not seen them, or else he cared little who witnessed his gaiety. He flicked the reins, and the sleigh bounded forward across the lawn, the lady clutching at his arm in mock alarm, her laughter ringing clear through the frosty air.

The sound seemed to echo in Merry's very chest. A wave of humiliation swept over her—hot and stinging, which seemed absurd against the cold. It was as though all her doubts of the past days had taken flesh and presented themselves before her eyes, daring her to deny them. The bracelet upstairs, the kiss that had left her cold, the whispers from the tavern—each accusation returned now with a companion in fur and ribbons.

Her mare tossed her head, feeling the hard grip of her rider's hand. Merry gathered the reins and turned sharply from the gate.

"I must go on," she said, her voice tight. She did not wait for Joshua's answer. She pressed the mare into a brisk trot, her skirts swaying and her chin high, as though she could ride away from what she had seen.

The beautiful morning had shattered. The light, that moments before had seemed to gild the fields, now mocked her. She heard still, in memory, the young woman's laughter beside Barnaby, so light and careless. It pierced her, though she told herself angrily it ought not. What right had he, if he meant to court her, to parade another in so familiar a fashion? And if he did not mean to court her—then what a fool she was.

Her cheeks burned. She urged the mare faster, wanting only to be away, to put distance between herself and that sleigh, from Joshua's silent company, from the treacherous hope that had filled her earlier in the ride.

She knew she should not care so much. She told herself, sternly, that it was nothing—a lark, a trifle, a scrap of winter amusement that meant no more than a snowball tossed by children. Yet the words rang false and hollow. Somewhere deep inside, she had wanted Barnaby's attentions to mean more. She had wanted to believe. And now the sight of him, so at ease, so gay with another lady, told her more than any whispered warning could have done.

The beautiful morning was ruined.

CHAPTER 8

*J*oshua would have spared Merry that scene if he could possibly have done so. The moment her chin lifted rigidly and the light went out of her eyes, he knew exactly how deep the cut had gone. Tremaine, on Lord Bruton's lawn, a sleek pair tossing their heads, a bright-eyed little beauty pressed close for warmth and laughter, obvious intimacy between the two of them. It was a tableau arranged to wound, even if by accident. Merry did not look at him. She did not need to. He saw her gather the reins and heard the decision in the quickened step of her mare. He let her go because pride sometimes needs speed more than company, and because if he had tried to hold her in that moment he would have said more than prudence could mend. He therefore followed at a polite distance.

Back at Wychwood, the day resumed its cheerful tyranny. Children tugged at his coat to show him the best of the slide they had made in the snow. Then he joined his brothers in chopping some wood, followed by his mother pressing a cup of chocolate into his hand and telling him he looked as he had at nine years old, when a Latin exercise had offended his sense of justice. He smiled when required and answered when spoken to, yet under all the bustle the image burned steadily of Merry's set mouth and that cursed scene.

By noon he had done everything he could do that involved muscle and little that involved speech. He went in search of quiet and found the library empty save for the smell of leather and the creak of winter in the panelling. A fire had been left alive, and he stood by it until his hands forgot the cold, thinking about the letter he had sent. He did not expect an answer from London so soon. The post did not fly. Yet hope, like a child, often runs to the door before it hears a knock.

The knock came sooner than sense would have predicted. Not an hour later the butler entered with a plain packet and that particular tilt of the head which meant a letter a man might prefer to receive without witnesses. Joshua broke the seal with measured carefulness. He knew the hand before he reached the signature. Renforth wrote as he spoke—briskly, with more truth than comfort.

MY DEAR FIELDING,

YOUR NOTE FINDS me in town when I wish to be elsewhere, and thus better placed to answer than my sins deserve. You ask for truth rather than scandal, so I will tell you what I know and what I infer.

Lord Bruton is a man I know well. He despairs of his son with an energy worthy of a better cause. The young gentleman's losses are heavy and deep. There were unpleasant scenes at two gaming houses in November and a very ugly whisper at a third, which I will not set down here.

His lordship has cut him off in everything but name and shelter. He took him into the country to get him out of sight of creditors and unsavoury companions. His statement, to at least three men of my acquaintance, is that the boy must marry fortune, and speedily, or he will be allowed to experience the inside of a sponging-house.

As to associates, your old seaman speaks no more than the truth. The lad has been in nefarious company. In your small Gloucestershire village, those who seek him will stand out like a rotting carcass.

Keep me informed on your side. I do not love being the author of ill news at Christmas, but I love the thought of a good girl being used worse still.

YOUR OBEDIENT, *etc.,*
  Renforth

JOSHUA READ it twice through and then once more, though nothing altered. He had asked for truth and been given it. Tremaine was driven by desperation. Lord Bruton had set him upon the country like a hound slipped from leash with only one scent in its nose: fortune. If the fellow smiled at Merry it was not because he had discovered a heart he had not known he possessed, but because her portion had presented itself as a remedy that did not taste of physic. Nevertheless, would Bruton tolerate such a *mésalliance*?

Joshua laid the letter upon the table and set his palms upon the wood on either side. Anger moved across him and was gone, leaving only the stubborn steadiness that had always done him more good. Anger would tempt a man into ungallant action. Steadiness would keep him from ruining everything with the right words at the wrong time.

He folded the letter and put it in his pocket. He took out paper and wrote a brief reply while the facts were still clear in his head.

My THANKS. Your candour is a kindness and will be used as best I am able. I will enquire here as quietly as I can. If you learn anything further, a second cruelty will be another favour.
  J.F.

HE SANDED AND SEALED IT. The action calmed him a little. Then the question that had been waiting since he had first thought to write to London came and stood in front of him and refused to move. How was he to tell Merry without making her hate him? There are truths that feel like contempt when they fall from the wrong mouth, and warnings that sound like jealousy even when they rise from care. He could produce evidence. He could name names. He could lay the thing out as neatly as a plan of attack, and still she might hear only, *I think you a fool and myself in the right of it.*

He went in search of his mother because she had never once mistaken his motives, even when he had been six and had cut his own hair with kitchen scissors in order to look more like a cavalry officer. He found her in the small parlour with her work-basket and a little regiment of stockings. She looked up at him and then down at the letter that he was aware had altered the set of his mouth. She put her mending aside at once.

"Well," she said. "You have been fed something bitter and are deciding whether it will do more good than harm to share it."

"Renforth writes," he said, and handed her the letter because his mother had earned the right to see what moved his face.

She read it with that tranquil speed she reserved for serious matters. There were only two places where her lips pressed together. She folded the paper along the crease he had made and gave it back to him.

"I had hoped you to be wrong," she said, very quietly.

"As had I."

"And now you intend to tell Merry." It was no query; she knew her son.

"I mean for her to know, if necessary. I do not mean to be foolish about it."

His mother's eyes were both kind and shrewd. "You cannot tell her as a man tells a girl. She is not a silly chit. You must tell her as one adult tells another adult he respects. If you face her being noble and long-suffering, she will want to lash out at you. If you make it a contest between you and Mr. Tremaine, she will defend the weaker argument out of stubbornness, which is a thing we both admire in her when it is not in the way of her future. Offer her facts and the confidence that she can bear them. Then stand out of her light."

"'Stand out of her light,'" he repeated, because the phrase struck home.

"Very likely she will resent you for a time," his mother went on. "However, she knows the taste of truth and she trusts you, though she does not yet thank you for it."

He drew breath. "If I were to speak first to Mr. Roxton?"

"You would wound her pride. A father must know, but let her be the one who takes it to him unless it becomes necessary. If you carry it, you will look like a man who wishes to fix a thing that is not his to mend."

He nodded. "Then the how must be as simple as the what."

"Choose your time and your place," she said. "And, Joshua—do not tell her what to do. She will hear orders even where you do not intend them."

He put a hand lightly upon her shoulder. "I will remember."

By the time he found Merry, however, it appeared he was too late.

Merry had just reached the drawing room when the butler appeared with a card upon a salver. His expression was as smooth as the silver from which the tray was fashioned, yet Merry thought she saw something like curiosity behind the polish. He came directly to her.

"Mr. Barnaby Tremaine," he announced, low enough for her ears alone, "asks if Miss Roxton will receive him for a few minutes."

She felt the ground tilt. Penelope's eyes flew to her face and then quickly away. The room had become suddenly large and far too bright.

"Thank you," Merry said. "Show him to the green salon."

The butler bowed and withdrew. Penelope caught her hand as if in play and gave it a quick press.

"Do you wish me to accompany you?" she asked under her breath.

Merry shook her head. "No. It is nothing. He comes to apologize for yesterday's folly, I am certain."

Penelope's mouth tightened as if she had tasted something sour. She did not speak the thought that stood rested in her face. She released Merry's hand and nodded once. The other ladies had not yet remarked on the exchange. Mrs. Fielding was laughing at something Mrs. Roxton had said about the vicar's sermon. The room's inhabitants carried on with their amusements.

Merry crossed the corridor. Her steps sounded louder than she liked, though she walked as she always walked. In the green salon the fire burned brightly. For an instant, she wished she could step into the grate and vanish up the chimney like smoke.

The door opened. Barnaby Tremaine came in with that smooth grace that could make even the act of closing a door seem a performance learned for an audience. He was very handsome in dark blue. His neckcloth was tied to a nicety.

"Merry," he said warmly, and then corrected himself with a bow. "Miss Roxton."

"Mr. Tremaine," she returned, offering her hand. He bent over it with the proper degree of respect. No one watching them would have guessed that only two evenings before, beneath the mistletoe, she had pushed him away. No one would have guessed that yesterday morning Penelope had reported a scene at the tavern that had made even the married ladies purse their lips, nor the scene from this morning. Merry herself had spent the day walking in the park and turning over painful thoughts like cold stones in a pocket. She had not decided what to do with them. Now the man who had set every thought in motion stood smiling at her as if the world were at peace.

"I am come to beg an indulgence," he began, taking the chair she indicated. "I was due at my father's table and stole away from yours like a man with no manners. I would repair that transgression, if you will allow me."

"You are here," she said, and tried to keep her tone even. "That repairs much."

He looked gratified. "You are goodness itself. If you knew how I have scolded myself. It is a cruel truth that Christmas-tide asks a gentleman to be in three places at once. A fellow does his best and still offends everywhere."

Merry folded her hands. She had thought to begin gently. The words that came out did not obey. "Who was the young lady in the sleigh with you this morning?"

He blinked. His smile shivered, then steadied. "You saw us?"

"I did. The lane below the rise turns an open curve. One cannot help but admire any equipage that takes it at such speed."

"Ah," he said lightly, though a muscle near his jaw stirred. "You will recall Mr. and Mrs. Dunning of Bruton Farm? Their second daughter, Miss Lydia Dunning, begged me for a turn. An old family acquaintance: a child almost. I could not deny her without seeming uncivil."

Merry kept her gaze upon him. She knew of no such family, but that was neither here nor there. "She did not look a child. She looked very pretty and very warm at your side."

Colour rose under his fine skin. "It was the only way to keep the blanket over her against the wind. The thing is nothing, I assure you. The Dunnings are respectable. You know how country folk think it a boon to have ridden with the Baron's son. I did not wish to disappoint a house that has always shown my family loyalty."

He spoke well. His tone held the exact balance of apology and charm that reduced many offences to air. Merry felt the old habit rise in her, the one that sought to excuse for the sake of peace. She pressed it down.

He leaned forward, hands outspread. "I am guilty of making a trifle look worse than it was. I cannot deny that—but indeed I meant no slight to you. If I had known you were there, I would have turned on the instant and introduced you. You must not put a weight upon it that it cannot bear."

She wished she did not hear, behind those words, the exact same phrase he had used about the bracelet. A trifle. Nothing more. She felt the box in her drawer as if it had been upon her wrist.

"And at the Crown?" she asked, before she could stop herself. "Penelope says her husband saw you at cards."

He laughed, a little too quickly. "Men always see one another at cards. It is their duty. There was nothing in it. We amused ourselves. Someone put a girl on my knee for a jest. The Crown is not Almack's, Miss Roxton. I cannot be held responsible for the way villagers choose to show their spirits."

Merry did not speak. He hurried on.

"You know how people talk. If a man wins he is a sharp. If he loses he is a rum-touch. I left before midnight and paid my markers. That is more than most can say in any room with a deck of cards. Pray think better of me."

He was good at sounding wounded by the very suspicion he had called upon himself. Merry looked at him across the narrow space and wished she had not seen what she had seen. It would be easier to be pleased if one were blind.

"Very well," she said at last, because she could not bear to quarrel. "I will think better of you today."

He exhaled as if the air had been fetched back into his chest. "You are an angel."

He changed subjects with the grace of a dancer. "I brought the bracelet yesterday in stupidity. I ought to have begged your father's leave first. I see that now. If you would entrust it to me, I will ask at once and return it properly. Or, if you prefer, I will take it back and bring something modest instead."

Merry had hidden the case as if it had been a sin. The thought of returning it to him now, in this room, made her heart bump. Yet keeping it felt worse. She shook her head.

"It is done now," she said. "We can do what is proper next time."

He looked baffled, then alarmed, then contrite. "You are right. I have handled the matter badly. I came today to put everything to rights. Miss Roxton—Merry—" He caught himself, as though the word had leaped up of its own accord. "Forgive me. I have rehearsed fine speeches and now cannot find one that does not sound foolish. Will you walk with me for two minutes where the door is in sight? I will not steal you past a chaperon. I wish only to say one thing without every servant listening."

She hesitated. The green room was safe and bright. The corridor beyond was empty. The great door stood at the far end with its holly wreath brave in the grey light. She inclined her head.

They walked only as far as the niche where a marble shepherdess watched a marble lamb with devotion. He stopped there and faced her. The change in his manner was quick. The polish did not vanish, but something inside it gave way to urgency.

"Merry," he said, his voice very low. "You must know I admire you above every lady I have ever met. Your sense, your spirit, your beauty. I have been clumsy and the village has eyes that enlarge everything. I will not pretend to be better than I am, but I can promise to try to be worthy of you. Will you do me the honour of accepting my hand?"

The words fell into the quiet with the exact weight she had thought to hear once upon a time. For an instant the world before her blurred at the edges. Was this what she had wanted?

He went on, soft and earnest. "I speak here because I would not put you to the pain of a public refusal should you not be ready. I would keep the engagement quiet for a very few days. I must have my father's blessing. I know how to approach him, and I would not have you see the business side of what ought to be wholly tender. Give me leave to tell him in my own fashion. I will then speak to your father with all respect. We shall be announced before Twelfth Night. I will not ask you to wait longer than that."

Her heart beat an odd beat, as if uncertain whether to rush or hold. He had said the words. He had asked. He had even pleaded a little. Her mind reached for the list of doubts she had written upon the air only this morning. The kiss that had felt like nothing. The bracelet called a trifle. The sight of a girl huddled up to him in the sleigh. The loss at cards. The way he made excuses and then took offence and then begged. Yet he was here now, and he was handsome and plausible and certain that the world would bend to arrange itself around them both. He had called her sense and spirit beautiful, which was not nothing.

"Why keep it secret?" she asked, although he had given her a reason. She wanted to hear it again to test its validity.

"Because I know my father," he said, with a little grimace that sat well on him. "He is a man who will ask to see your portion first. I will not have him insulting you with figures when I can oblige him to remember he has a heart. Give me three days to manage him and then I will stand you before him and make him thank me for the honour."

The words were artful, yet they struck true. She knew enough of fathers to believe he might be right. However, she did not wish to stand to be valued like sugar. If three days could remove such ugliness, did that not recommend them?

"And you do me the honour," he said again, his voice lower still, "of believing that nothing would make me prouder than to see you mistress of my house."

A weakness ran through her. To be the mistress of a lord's residence was a cherished dream, she thought. For long enough had she wished to step from this narrow village into a wider world in which she might do good, in which she might be seen, in which she might become a wife and mother.

She lifted her eyes and met his. They were bright with a triumph held carefully back, as one dams a stream for a ceremony and then lets it run. She heard herself say, very quietly, "Yes."

He caught her hands. He did not kiss her again. "You make me the happiest man in Gloucestershire," he said.

"Three days," she said, because she must be seen to command something.

"Three," he agreed. "I shall go to my father at once, then I will request an interview with Mr. Roxton. Until then we must keep our good fortune a secret between ourselves."

"Of course."

He pressed her hands and let them go. "I do not deserve you," he said. "I shall spend a lifetime attempting to prove I do."

He left her there, by the marble shepherdess, with a bow. The door closed behind him. The tread of his boots faded down the corridor.

Merry stood very still until she could hear the clock in the hall count two slow minutes. Then she walked back into the green drawing room and sat down in the chair she had left. She placed her hands upon her lap. They trembled and she did not wish them to. She clasped them until the tremble became less.

She told herself she had done a sensible thing. She had accepted a man of good family who had asked for her with respect. She had granted him three days to arrange family matters in a way that would spare both houses discomfort. There was nothing in it that a sensible woman would refuse. A world of safety had opened, with a door that bore her name. She only had to walk through. The trouble was that safety felt like a room with too little air.

CHAPTER 9

Joshua went in search of Merry with the idea of finding a moment alone. The house had entered that bustling restlessness which followed breakfast at Christmas-tide, when plans were made or discarded with cheer. He meant to ask for ten minutes of her time, intending to give no speeches and no warnings, only reassurance.

The corridor to the green saloon lay empty when he reached it. The winter light fell in a thin square across the carpet. He took two steps and then halted. Voices, low and urgent, came from the room.

Joshua knew at once whose voices they were. Barnaby Tremaine's tones were smooth and persuasive.

"Will you walk with me for two minutes where the door is in sight? I will not steal you past a chaperon. I wish only to say one thing without every servant listening."

Joshua did not move. It was not virtue that kept him still. It was the battlefield instinct which tells a man to see exactly what is happening before he charges into it. He took a breath and let it out silently. If he turned now, his boots would ring on the boards and his retreat would be louder than a declaration.

"Merry," Tremaine went on, bringing his voice down to a whisper.

"You must know I admire you above every lady I have ever met. Your sense, your spirit, your beauty. I have been clumsy and the village has eyes that enlarge everything. I will not pretend to be better than I am, but I can promise to try to be worthy of you. Will you do me the honour—"

Joshua's heart lurched. He could not see Merry past the angle of the alcove, only the movement of Tremaine's dark coat and the tilt of his head as he bent closer to press the advantage he had made for himself. It felt like watching a comrade go down in the smoke twelve paces away, too far to reach in time. What had his silver-forked tongue said to make her forgive his behaviour?

Joshua told himself there was still a world of difference between being asked and being won. He told himself she might refuse. He told himself anything that would keep him where he stood and not send him blundering forward into a scene and make everything worse. Tremaine continued on and Joshua could not make out the words. Then he heard Merry speak.

Her voice was clear, though low. "Why must it be secret?"

"Because I know my father," he said, with a little grimace. "He is a man who will ask to see your portion first. I will not have him insulting you with figures when I can oblige him to remember he has a heart. Give me three days to manage him and then I will stand you before him and make him thank me for the honour."

There was a pause that bit into Joshua's chest like frost. When Merry spoke again, the single syllable seemed to strike the wainscotting and return to him in a shape larger than itself.

"Yes."

He closed his eyes. The word gave him no right to move or intervene. He pressed his palm hard against the cool wood of the panelling, as if to remind his body it still had a wall to lean on. When he opened his eyes he saw, reflected in the glass opposite, Tremaine's figure bow with triumph held in check and Merry's face lifted, pale and composed. He could not read her eyes in that thin reflection. He did not need to. He knew the look she wore when she had done a difficult thing as if it were nothing.

He stepped back soundlessly until he reached a bend in the corridor and then walked swiftly but without evident haste. The house swallowed him. Voices came and went. Some child laughed with the kind of sudden explosive joy that told of victory at a game. Joshua kept his pace even and his face free of the tumult within.

He went to the library for solace, but it offered none. He stood with both hands upon the back of a chair until his breathing settled. Then he let the first wild rush of anger and despair pass through him and out again.

He could not think of Merry as lost—not yet. It was not too late until the vows were said before God and the register signed. A secret engagement was not a sacrament. It was a thread that could be cut by truth if truth were revealed properly. He had no wish to triumph. He had every wish that she be spared a life that would grind her spirit to dust while people admired her title and her jewels.

He sat down soberly and put his head in his hands, not because he was beaten, but because he needed to act quickly yet with caution. If he blundered now, if he came to her with facts that sounded as though he was merely intent on proving himself right, he would deserve the contempt she would hand him—and the marriage he could not prevent.

How miserable would she be, tied to what lay beneath that handsome coat and those practised compliments?

Merry, with her love of mornings and lambing pens and the clean honesty of a day's work, would be crushed. The best of her would either grow bitter or hide itself. She would still smile. She would still be herself in company. But the private person—her spirit would be crushed.

Abruptly, he stood up and paced the length of the Turkish carpet. Should he approach her? Yes—but how? She had given her word. He would not ask her to break it lightly or make of himself the villain in the story. All at once, he must be near enough to catch her if she stumbled and far enough to let her choose the path. It was a hard business, but hard business was what he knew.

Very well. He would go on gathering the truth quietly to have ready the moment she reached for it. He would make himself the safest person to come to when she needed someone. She must know he wanted her happiness more than any victory. Later he would examine why he felt so intensely.

The library door opened a crack. His mother's face appeared in the gap, her eyes as quick as a bird's. She read him in one glance.

"Well?" she said. "I saw her return to the drawing room looking shaken."

"She has given her word to keep a secret," he answered, which told his mother all she needed.

"For how long?"

"He asked for three days."

Mrs. Fielding entered and shut the door softly behind her. "Then we shall be particularly occupied for three days."

"Doing what, precisely?"

"You are to continue exactly as you have been, giving her your attentions," she said. "A woman does not change her mind in something like this without good cause and an alternative."

"Am I to stand silent with damning proof that would only cause her future to be misery?"

"No, of course not." His mother frowned.

"If she asks me for particulars—?"

"You will give them, briefly and without relish," his mother said. "You will not make a sermon of them. 'Twould be best for her to discover on her own."

He nodded. "But there is very little time."

"Then you had best busy yourself in showing her the better alternative."

She turned and left before he could argue that he was not searching for a wife.

THE NEXT MORNING dawned sharp and bright, the snow crisping underfoot as the household made its way to church. Every church morning was much the same—bells chiming, children's laughter echoing down the lane, breath misting like smoke in the cold—but that morning felt different to Merry. Her heart was uncertain, her thoughts too crowded. This was not the way a newly betrothed young lady should feel.

She had scarcely slept. The memory of Barnaby's low, persuasive voice—keep it secret, my love, only for a few days—had tangled itself with dreams until she woke half convinced she had betrayed herself. Now, walking between her mother and Penelope, she pressed her muff close and told herself sternly that she should be happy. She was promised. She ought to glow with contentment.

Yet contentment refused to come.

The bells of St. Mary's rang out across the valley, calling the faithful like silver hounds on a scent. The church stood golden and ancient against the blue morning sky, its steeple piercing the pale clouds. Villagers hurried along the lane in their Sunday best—bonnets trimmed with holly and boys in patched coats, grinning through the cold. It had always filled Merry with a kind of humble joy. Today it felt like stepping onto a stage.

Inside, the warmth of candles and bodies filled the air with that familiar mixture of beeswax and spice. The Roxtons took their customary pew near the front. The Fieldings gathered, a picture of good-natured disorder, with Joshua helping the children divest themselves of scarves and cloaks. His hair caught the candlelight. For one breath, Merry forgot to worry.

And then the stir began.

The Bruton carriage had arrived. The vicar himself straightened in the vestry doorway as though expecting royalty. The congregation turned slightly, heads tilting like flowers following the sun.

Lord and Lady Bruton entered first—imposing, wrapped in furs, heads held high. Their countenances were the perfect mixture of piety and condescension. Their pew, naturally, stood nearest the altar, draped with cushions embroidered with the family crest.

But it was not Lord or Lady Bruton who drew the whispered interest of the congregation. It was those who came behind.

Barnaby Tremaine led a young lady by the arm—a lady Merry knew at once, though she had prayed she might be mistaken. The same beauty from the sleigh, her bonnet pale blue to match the ribbons trailing from her muff. The girl's laughter, low and musical, floated across the quiet church like perfume.

Merry's breathing stopped.

Her first thought was disbelief. Her second, foolishly, was that perhaps Barnaby had not seen her, but of course he had. His gaze passed across the pews with the faintest flicker of awareness before he bowed to Lady Bruton and guided his companion gracefully into the family pew beside him. He looked entirely at ease, as though escorting one lady one day and proposing to another the next were nothing worth remark.

The congregation settled, though the air seemed thicker for all the whispers it held. The vicar began the service, his voice as sonorous as ever, but Merry heard scarcely a word. Her pulse thrummed in her ears.

Who was the young woman? Barnaby had told her the lady in the sleigh was a mere tenant's daughter, but no tenant dressed in such finery, nor carried herself with such easy confidence. The ribbons on her bonnet were silk—London silk—and the fur about her shoulders could not have come from any Gloucestershire market.

Was it all a lie, then? Every word?

Her hands tightened within her skirts.

Joshua sat beside her, as solemn and steady as ever, his eyes fixed upon the vicar. He sang the hymns in his low voice. It always seemed to find the right note without effort. She envied him that steadiness—envied how little the world seemed to shake him. She wondered if he had noticed. He must have noticed. How could anyone fail to see the way the young lady leaned close to whisper to Barnaby, how she smiled up at him from beneath her lashes, how his answering look held the faint indulgence of a man used to being adored?

Heat burned behind Merry's eyes; part shame, part fury.

Her mother touched her arm gently when it came time to stand for the reading. "Are you feeling unwell, my dear?"

"No, Mama," she whispered. Her voice felt brittle, as though one more word might shatter it.

Joshua turned his head slightly, his gaze resting on her for a heartbeat before returning to his prayer book. He said nothing. He never said anything unnecessary. Yet something in his look—so calm, so knowing—made her cheeks flame. He must have guessed. He must know how wretched she felt.

The sermon droned on. The Bruton pew glittered like a tableau of privilege. Lord Bruton stared straight ahead, his expression carved from marble. The lady beside Barnaby leaned nearer still, her gloved hand brushing his sleeve as she whispered something that made him smile—a slow, indulgent smile Merry remembered too well.

Merry fixed her gaze on the altar and prayed, not for patience or understanding, but simply to be invisible.

When the final hymn rose—'Hark! The Herald Angels Sing'—she sang too loudly, desperate to drown the ache in her chest. Joshua's deep voice joined hers, steady and sure, a sound like earth under her feet. Yet she felt only humiliation.

When the service ended, the congregation spilled into the churchyard, bright with frost and chatter. Lord Bruton's party moved through them like a miniature procession. Merry watched, unable to stop herself. Barnaby bowed to Lady Bruton, handed the beauty into the waiting carriage, and only then turned to acknowledge Merry's presence across the path—with a polite inclination of the head, no more.

No warmth. No familiarity. Nothing that could betray the secret he had pressed upon her only yesterday.

She stared at him, willing him to offer some explanation, some hint of apology. He merely smiled, thin and distant, before turning away to assist his mother into the carriage. The door shut with a soft, final sound.

Joshua appeared beside her then, his voice quiet as he spoke. "The frost is biting. Allow me to see you home."

She nodded mutely. The words she wished to speak—to scream, perhaps—stuck fast in her throat. As they walked down the lane, she could hear the jingle of the Bruton carriage fading into the distance, at once both cheerful and cruel.

Joshua said nothing more, but his silence was the kind that waited for her to speak when she could.

Merry, however, could not yet bear it. In her heart, she knew the truth. Nothing was worth being tied to someone who would not acknowledge her—but how to extricate herself? If only she could unburden herself to someone, but she had given her word. To betray that secret now would be to confess her foolishness to the entire world.

They walked in silence, side by side, falling behind the others. Merry drew her cloak closer and fixed her eyes on the ground. At last, unable to bear the weight between them, she found her courage. Her voice came small at first, then firmer.

"Do you wish to say something about Tremaine's inconstancy?"

Joshua's expression did not change. He clasped his hands behind his back and took several measured steps before answering, as though each word required its proper distance.

"I wish nothing of the sort," he said at length. "I want only your happiness, Merry."

She stopped walking. The cold air clouded between them. "My happiness," she repeated, half in disbelief. "Even when I have made such a fool of myself?"

His gaze met hers, steady and gentle. "Especially then."

Her throat tightened. He was too kind. His composure, his restraint, made her feel suddenly young and small and, unbearably, seen as such. "You must think me very foolish," she whispered.

"I think," he said quietly, "that anyone with a generous heart may sometimes be deceived by the appearance of generosity in another. A moment of blindness does not make a fool of anyone. It makes them human."

She blinked hard, the frozen air stinging her eyes. "A generous sentiment." Merry glanced sideways at him, her heart heavy yet a little lighter for his company. Unfortunately the situation was not so simple.

CHAPTER 10

How Joshua wished Merry would confide in him and he could ease her burden. The restraint it cost him to remain silent was almost a physical pain. Every look, every quiet word from Merry seemed to ask something of him, and yet not the one thing he wanted her to ask. She had pride enough for ten men. She would fight to the last inch of self-respect before admitting that Barnaby Tremaine's attentions had cut her to the quick.

Joshua could not bear the thought of her discovering Tremaine's perfidy in some public way—of being made a spectacle by his deceit. Better by far that she hear it from him, he reflected, even if she despised him for saying it. And yet, he remembered his mother's counsel.

No, he must not speak—unless she invited it.

He could act, however. He could discover who the lady was upon Tremaine's arm that morning at church, the same young beauty who had ridden beside him in the sleigh. Joshua was almost certain now that Tremaine was playing both young ladies false, his confidence built upon a gambler's instinct that one of the fortunes would fall his way. He had seen men like that before, in London parlours and in camp tents. They thrived on risk and did not care who was hurt along the way.

Joshua clinched his teeth. The difference now was that the stakes were not money, but Merry.

And Merry was no man's second prize.

Still, Joshua's tortured thoughts continued, he could not expose Tremaine without proof. If the young lady belonged to another family of means, then there might be whispers in the village or something to be gleaned from the vicar's wife, whose knowledge of lineage rivalled Debrett's. He would begin his inquiries discreetly—it was his occupation, after all. For today, however, he would do something simpler: he would make Merry smile again.

The ice on the lower lake had been declared sound that morning, and the children were clamouring to skate. It was an occupation that left little room for brooding, and if he could coax Merry onto the ice, perhaps she might forget—for a time—about Tremaine's intolerable behaviour that morning.

The lake lay in a hollow at the edge of the park, ringed by bare willows, the slender branches of which glimmered with frost. The sky was that clean winter blue that promises both sunlight and cold in equal measure. The Fielding and Roxton children were already careering across the surface like a barrage of cannon-balls. Their shrieks of delight echoed against the frozen banks.

Joshua arrived with a coil of rope and a sense of readiness like a good soldier, born more from experience than optimism. No family expedition near a frozen body of water had ever gone entirely without incident.

Merry was there too, of course, her cheeks bright beneath the edge of her fur-lined hood, her skates slung over her arm. She was laughing with Penelope's little boy, who was determined to tie his own laces despite the evidence of three failed attempts. The sight of her—alive with motion, her hair escaping its pins—struck Joshua with sudden, quiet force.

"Uncle Joshua!" cried Roger, sliding perilously near to his knees.

"You must come—Father says you can skate faster than anyone in the army!"

"That," said Joshua dryly, "is because the army pays us to run from danger."

Merry looked up then, her eyes bright with mischief. "You always did run faster than the rest of us, even when we were children. If I recall correctly, you pushed me straight into the hedge when you tried to pass me on the pond."

"I did no such thing," he said, feigning outrage. "You fell of your own accord."

"You tripped me," she insisted, her tone all mock severity, "and I have never forgiven you."

"You forgive easily enough," he said, a smile tugging at his mouth. "You proved it five minutes later by pelting me with snow until I begged for mercy."

Her laughter warmed the cold air. "I might be persuaded to repeat that victory."

"Not before a rematch, surely?"

Her brows lifted in challenge. "Do you wish to race with me?"

"I do. Although you may recall the result from the last occasion."

"Indeed I do," she said, fastening her skates with brisk efficiency. "You lost."

"I allowed you to win, Miss Roxton. You were ten, and my honour could withstand the defeat."

"Then it will not survive today," she said, rising gracefully. "Children, you shall judge!"

At once, half a dozen small faces turned eagerly toward them, and a chorus of "Race! Race!" filled the frosted air. Joshua sighed, knowing full well he had sealed his fate.

They set off side by side, their skates cutting clean arcs across the ice. Merry moved with speed and confidence, her cloak flaring behind her like a crimson banner. He followed close, her laughter floating back to him—bright, reckless…and free. For a few glorious moments, he forgot the heaviness that had been sitting upon him for days. He was not Captain Fielding, soldier or spy, but the boy who had once chased a laughing girl across a winter pond and thought her the very definition of joy.

When they reached the far end of the lake, she spun sharply and came to a stop in a spray of ice. "Admit it," she said, breathless but triumphant. "You cannot beat me."

He came to a halt beside her, smiling despite himself. "Perhaps not, but it is a race I would gladly lose again."

She laughed, the sound soft and unguarded. For that moment she seemed herself again—spirited, radiant and untouched by care. Joshua, watching her, thought with a pang how fiercely he wished to keep her that way.

If he had to stand between her and disappointment, between her and the man who would wound her pride for sport, he would do it without hesitation. For now, though, he said nothing of Tremaine, nothing of secrets or scandal. He would let her laugh, and skate, and forget the weight she carried—if only for a single winter morning.

The cheers of their race had no sooner died away than the boys, flushed with excitement, clamoured for their own.

"Let us try!" cried Roger, his nose pink and eyes bright. "Uncle Joshua must race us all the way to the willows and back. Last one across the line is a coward!"

Joshua laughed. "A coward? You had better skate faster than your tongue, young man."

Within moments, half a dozen boys were lined up upon the ice, their faces alight with anticipation. Merry joined the girls at the edge, calling good-natured encouragement. Joshua crouched with the others.

"Ready!" shouted Merry. "Go!"

They flew forward in a cloud of frost. Joshua hung back slightly, unwilling to rob them of victory but determined to keep watch. Arthur, the youngest, lagged behind at first, but spurred on by laughter and pride, began to push harder, his small legs churning the ice in uneven strokes.

Halfway across, Joshua saw it—the faint ridge of thawed snow refrozen into a shallow seam. He shouted a warning, but Roger's momentum was too great. The boy's skate caught, and he went sprawling forward with a cry, landing hard upon his arm.

Merry gasped and was on the ice almost before Joshua reached the child. The boy sat hunched, teeth clenched, his face pale beneath the rosy glow of play.

"It's his wrist," Joshua said at once, dropping to one knee. He brushed away the snow and examined the small, trembling hand with practised precision. "Clean break, I'll wager. We will need to set it straight away before the swelling begins."

Merry knelt beside him, her expression calm though her breath came fast. "Tell me what to do."

He glanced at her briefly, meeting those clear, resolute eyes. "Hold his shoulder firmly. I will straighten it quickly."

She nodded, tightening her hold about the boy's upper arm, murmuring soothing nonsense into his ear. "There now, Roger, brave boy, look at me—not at him. Keep your eyes on mine."

Joshua took the wrist in both hands, his grip sure but gentle. "One breath in, lad," he said quietly, "and let it out." On the exhale, he drew the limb into alignment with one swift motion. Roger cried out, but held still.

"Well done," Joshua murmured. "The worst of it is over."

Merry exhaled shakily, colour returning to her cheeks. "You did that as if you had done it a hundred times."

"More than I care to count," he said, giving her a faint smile. "Soldiers are forever breaking something. The trick is to do it quickly before they realize what you are going to do."

She tore her scarf from around her neck without hesitation. "Here—use this to keep it still."

Together they worked efficiently, Joshua fashioning a rough splint from two stout twigs fetched by a nearby boy and binding them with Merry's scarf. Their movements fell into a rhythm—his steadiness and her care combined seamlessly. When it was done, Roger managed a watery grin.

"There, now," Merry said, brushing a curl from his forehead. "No more heroics for today. You shall dine like a king tonight for your bravery."

Joshua lifted the child easily into his arms, feeling the weight of the small body settle against his shoulder. Merry skated beside him, steadying the boy's head against the jostling.

"You are very good with them," she said softly as they crossed the snow.

"Experience," he replied. "Half my regiment were still boys."

She looked up at him then, eyes bright with quiet admiration. "You make even the worst of things seem manageable."

He met her gaze and felt something stir, more dangerous than gratitude. He only hoped that when the time came to reveal Tremaine's perfidy, she could still admire something about him.

THREE DAYS HAD DRAGGED by since Sunday with no word, no sighting, no visit from Mr. Tremaine. In a place as small as Wychwood, silence was never simply quiet—it was a kind of noise all its own, humming with what was not said. Merry found she could not abide it another moment. If she sat in the morning room, the clock beat out anxieties with every tick. If she walked in the park, the bare trees seemed to hold their breath as she passed. She could not ride, because the ice was treacherous on the north path, and she did not trust her temper upon an icy lane, nor would she risk her horse. And so, out of stubbornness as much as sense, she took herself where heat and work might conquer useless feeling: into the kitchens to bake.

It was New Year's Eve. The house smelt of evergreens and beeswax and the scent of pies baking. Copper pans hung from their hooks, and the range glowed with flame. Mrs. Dempsey, the cook, ruled the room with curt orders. Two scullery maids darted to and fro with pans and pails. Someone laughed in the corridor and a footman's whistle came and went, cheerful and just shy of impertinence. It was a world of purpose. Merry loved it for that.

"Miss Merry!" cried Mrs. Dempsey when she entered with her

sleeves already rolled to her elbows. "You'll turn your hands to butter in here, you will. The heat would melt a statue."

"I shall risk it," Merry said, tying on an apron. "I mean to make biscuits, if you please."

Mrs. Dempsey's eyebrows climbed, pleased and suspicious at once. "You are always welcome, though the making of biscuits is a servant's task, to be sure."

"Then let me be a servant for an hour," Merry returned, and there must have been something in her tone that made Mrs. Dempsey stop looking for the pretty reason and settle for the honest one.

"Well, then—your chocolate's there," she said briskly, pointing with her floury elbow, "and your sugar there. Beat the eggs well. You will need more flour. Bess, fetch another bowl for Miss Merry—no, the big one."

Merry smiled and set to. The ritual soothed her. She had been a nuisance to their own cook at times, she was sure, but that lady allowed her to help when Merry needed something to do. She measured flour into the great bowl—two pounds, then a third. She added three ounces of salt, and one pound of sugar as Mrs. Saxby had taught her when she was twelve and determined to master the art. She cut in cold butter by hand, rubbing until the mixture looked like snow rubbed with sunlight.

Then she used a wooden spoon, relishing the familiar effort in the shoulder and wrist as the whole came together. When the spoon could do no more, she turned the dough onto the table and worked it with both hands until it yielded—not sticky, not dry, just the right texture. It felt as though she were kneading her impatience into something that might bear being near other people.

"Roll it thinner than your temper, my dear," Mrs. Dempsey advised, passing her the rolling pin. "Then cut us angels and stars. The little ones like the shapes."

"The little ones shall have them," Merry said, setting the pin to the dough. The first pass spread it smooth, while the second took shape.

"Miss Merry bakes like a dream," declared Daisy, the younger scullery maid, bobbing past with a pan of peeled potatoes and eyes like saucers. "I wish I could make them as even."

"You shall," Merry said, with cheer she manufactured on purpose. "It is only practice—and not eating half the paste."

Daisy giggled and darted away. Merry kept her eyes upon the biscuits. It would have made no difference had she stuffed her ears with fruit cake. Gossip in a country house was as sure as the sunrise. Two laundry maids came in with a basket of clothes, talking in low, fast tones. Mrs. Dempsey told them to hush and they hushed, which only made it worse, for they began to whisper, which rang louder than normal voices. Merry's ears centred on every word.

"Lord Bruton's house has gone through sugar like sand this week," said Bess, the other scullery maid, working a whisk with elegance. "Cook says their people fetched more from Cheltenham yesterday. There's company."

"Quality company," Daisy breathed, arranging plates, "with a London sound to them. I heard it at noon in the yard—'my lord' this, 'my lady' that. The new lot came Monday night. Cousins maybe."

"Not cousins," said Tom, a footman, appearing with the coal scuttle and the air of a man who knows everything. "Lord Dunning and his daughter. Saw their coach myself. The arms were as plain as daylight—three ravens and a cross. That's Dunning, sure enough."

Merry took the first tray from the oven, then took the tin cutters—a star, a bell, and the angel—and pressed them down in neat lines. She lifted each shape to a waiting tin, spacing them with a care she hoped would keep her from bursting into tears for no good reason at all.

"Dunning?" Daisy repeated, blinking. "But Miss—what was her name? The one in the blue bonnet—?"

Merry's hands faltered over a bell-shaped biscuit. She set it down and picked up a star instead, as if changing the shape of the thing could change the words' meaning.

"Lady Lydia Dunning," Tom supplied with relish, as if he had memorized the syllables expressly to deliver them in a kitchen. "A tidy piece, by what I saw. Lord Dunning's girl and neighbour in London to

Lord Bruton himself. Like as not the families dine together often when they're in residence."

Tremaine's damsel was not a tenant's chit, then.

"Lord Bruton wants a marriage made," Tom went on, lowering his voice even as he swelled with the importance of knowing. "He wants it set up quick. His lordship's boy has got wagers in half the houses from Bond Street to St. James's, so they say, and he means to mend it with a wife who brings money."

"Her father will be cautious," Mrs. Dempsey observed, as though she had not just rebuked them. "A father with sense is always slow, more's the pity for the foolish. He will have heard the talk."

"He has," Tom said, to his own satisfaction. "My cousin's wife's brother sells candles next to a coffee-house where the clerks all read the papers out loud and call it improving their minds. The talk there says Lord Dunning's not easy. Says he dislikes Mr. Tremaine for his cards and fast ways. He won't promise anything yet."

"Out," Mrs. Dempsey said, and flicked her towel at him. "You'll drop ash in my dough when you get puffed up with knowing. Go on, tell the footmen they shall have sugared biscuits if they fetch baskets from the dairy without breaking the handles."

Tom fled, grinning. The kitchen's hum shifted into a higher key, like a pot reaching the boil. Merry stood very straight for a moment, biscuit cutter in hand, while the world arranged itself into a new, uglier sense.

Lydia Dunning. Barnaby had not lied about her name. He had only neglected to mention the little matter of her father's title. A family friend, yes. A tenant, no. A neighbour in London, no less, which meant long acquaintance, easy habits, the same social sphere. No wonder Lydia Dunning had been sitting so close to him in the pew. No wonder Barnaby had looked indulgent, as if intimacy were familiar.

No wonder he had not introduced her. He had said—what had he said?—that he would present Merry to his father when the matter had been arranged. He had been eager to keep her secret. It struck her then, as sharply as the edge of the tin star in her fingers, that secrets might be kept for more than one convenience at a time.

The biscuit she held broke under her hand. She stared at the jagged half-star and laughed, a sound that startled even her. She gathered the scrap, and ground it hard onto the table, hard, as if pressure could force the truth into a shape that suited.

Mrs. Dempsey came to stand at her shoulder, not intrusively, only near. "You are working that like it were the devil himself," she said after a moment, her manner as mild as milk.

Merry eased her hands at once and blinked, brought back from the edge of something frayed and unhelpful. "Indeed I am," she remarked, and softly set the broken biscuit down.

They laid two trays with neat shapes. Merry brushed them with milk and a dust of sugar until they shone.

In the cool minute between tasks, conversation resumed as conversation always does when work allows it—the soft domestic current that makes a house a village.

"I will take the next trays," Merry said, reaching for the scraps and turning them without resentment now, because she had found a thing she could control. Her mind marched, however unwillingly, with what she had learned. Lord Bruton wanted Lydia Dunning. Lord Dunning was reluctant, but reluctance was not refusal. Barnaby Tremaine could be charming and was, in all likelihood, even now softening the Earl. It was clear what Lady Lydia wished for. Meanwhile Barnaby had engineered an engagement that lived in a little box with a ribbon around it and could be kept or put away as his prospects arranged themselves.

It was an ugly thought. Worse, indeed, was the fact it rang true.

"You'll burn your fingers," Daisy warned, passing with a rack. "Here—use the cloth."

The aroma of warm chocolate rose richer by the minute, curling around the room. She was grateful to be distracted. For that span of time she belonged to the ordinary magic of turning a bowl of common things into a comfort.

Yet even comfort did not abolish thought. While she sifted a little extra powdered sugar to fall upon the cooling biscuits, her mind churned.

No wonder he would not introduce her. No wonder he had asked for secrecy. No wonder he had looked through her in the churchyard as if she were a familiar piece of furniture he could claim when it suited him. If Lord Dunning could be persuaded, Merry's fortune would become an alternative at best, to be applied if his other prospect failed.

Heat rose in her face at the insult of it. Then, just as quickly, shame followed—shame at being surprised. Had she not known some of this already? Had not Joshua—without words, without any ungenerous triumph—warned her? Barnaby's words had been satin, but his actions were plain cloth. She was nothing to him but a last resort.

She placed three stars upon a plate and dusted them as if she were blessing them. She would not cry in a kitchen full of servants.

"Mama will want these for the tea-table," she said, because she had to say something, "and the nursery must have their share or they will storm the larder."

"They will storm the larder regardless," Mrs. Dempsey said with a fond smile. "Why do you not take a plateful up, Miss Merry?"

Merry laughed, the sound small and grateful. She set aside a dozen for the nursery and arranged the rest on a good plate for the parlour, the little pale crystals of sugar catching light through the window. As she turned, the back door opened and a gust of honest winter shouldered in, bringing with it Joshua Fielding.

Her humiliation only wanted this, she thought bitterly. Joshua had been right all along. She had to escape because she could not allow him to see how much the betrayal hurt.

CHAPTER 11

$\mathcal{A}$ letter from London lay on Joshua's dressing-table, brittle with cold where the footman had slipped it under his door at first light. He recognized Renforth's hand at once. He broke the seal and read the missive while standing, the fire at his back.

My dear Fielding,

I have it from two separate quarters that Lord Bruton is intent upon a match for his son with a young lady of fortune. The family name is Dunning. You will know of it if you read beyond the first page of the Chronicle.

The father is not eager, for reasons any man might claim who has heard of Tremaine's activities. He knows of the debts and has smelled the cards. He hesitates, but fathers have been persuaded into worse by peers who talk of duty, estates, and the necessity of propping up titles that have leaned too hard for too long.

In short: the boy is to be provided for at the expense of a fortune. If your Gloucestershire business touches the honour of any lady, I would have her warned—by fact if possible, by inference if you must. I wish I might offer proof.

Yours sincerely,
Renforth

JOSHUA READ it twice and folded it back to its original form. There was the truth, in black and white, the London shape of what they had tasted here in the country: a man to be mended with money, a father who mistook marriage for a son's improvement, a name to be shored up with a dowry as one props a wall with a timber and pretends it will stand through the next storm.

It altered nothing he already believed, yet he still sought proof. He thought of Merry's face in the church, the way she had looked straight ahead and forged onward. He had told himself he would not speak until she asked. He had also told himself he would have the truth ready when she did.

He dressed and took himself to the stables rather than to breakfast, leaving word for his mother that he had business in the village. Brutus stamped in the yard, his breath steaming patiently. Joshua mounted and rode out beneath the quiet sky, feeling the cold in his bones.

Besides the tavern, the grocer was the hub of news and gossip. He doubted any letters would arrive for him there, but it was as good an excuse as any to look in.

"Good morning, Mrs. Tanner. Have any letters arrived for the manor today?"

The postmistress, Mrs. Tanner, shook her head with a smile and a few cheerful remarks about the coming festivities. Joshua thanked her and turned to go when two farmers' wives came in behind him, shaking melted snow from their cloaks. They were already deep in conversation.

"...and Lord Bruton's cook says they have had the Dunnings down from London—his lordship's own doing, she said. The young lady is to be settled before spring. A match with Mr. Tremaine, if you please, though they say her father has misgivings—what with his debts and the talk of cards and women..."

Joshua paused, his hand tightening on his gloves. Dunning was the name Renforth had written in his letter—the girl's family. So it was true. Lord Bruton was parading his guest's daughter as a prize mare, while Tremaine, no doubt, meant to secure whichever fortune would have him first, to keep the moneylenders at bay.

He bought drops of peppermint for the children, nodded a farewell to the gossiping matrons, and left.

By the time he returned to Wychwood, his thoughts had settled into grim order. Having left Brutus in the care of a groom, he crossed the courtyard to enter the kitchen, warm and fragrant with spice. There stood Merry, her sleeves rolled up, her hands dusted with flour and a curl escaping her bonnet as she bent over a tray of biscuits.

He might have watched her for a full minute longer, content simply to admire the ordinary miracle of competence, but other voices found him.

"…I tell you it is true," a maid was whispering by the hearth. "Lord Dunning's own daughter. I saw them in church. She sat so near Mr. Tremaine, you would have thought she were in danger of falling off the seat if he did not prop her up with his arm."

"And me sister is the parlour maid at the manor. She said there is a betrothal brewing between Lady Lydia and the son."

"Hush, you," Cook hissed, clapping a spoon against her palm. "Mind your tongues. There is a lady at the table who need hear none of your cleverness."

Silence followed, but too late. Merry had stilled. She set down the biscuit-cutter with a care that turned the act into a ceremony, brushed her hands on her apron as if they were dusted by more than flour, and looked up without looking at any one of them. Joshua could not have named the expression in that first instant—shame, hurt, acceptance?— only that it struck him like a cry muffled in linen.

Merry straightened slowly and set down the biscuits she had been holding. She murmured to one of the kitchen maids—Joshua could not hear the words but her voice trembled at the edges. Then she turned and fled through the scullery door into the yard, the sound of her boots fading across the stones.

"Poor lass," Cook murmured, watching her go. "Something is

teasing her this morning. Pale as milk, she is, and working herself to the bone for no good reason."

Joshua's throat tightened. He knew what was teasing her—a parcel of truth, wrapped in gossip and bitterness.

For a moment, he considered going after her, but pride was a stubborn creature, and he doubted she would thank him for finding her with tears in her eyes. He, too, knew what it was to need the dignity of solitude when one's world shifted. No—'twas far better to give her time.

He turned away and stepped into the corridor.

The noise of boots and laughter met him at once—his brothers gathering in the front hall with their father and Mr. Roxton, the air alive with talk of the day's shoot.

"There he is!" cried Aaron, his cheeks ruddy from the cold already. "Come, Joshua, we are for the lower covers. The pheasants are fat and lazy after Christmas, and we have been ordered to bring back our supper."

"Indeed," Caleb added, handing Joshua a spare fowling piece. "You have no excuse, Brother—unless you mean to sit indoors with the ladies and the children."

Joshua forced a smile, taking the gun. "I should hate to deprive you of your best shot."

Their father appeared then, adjusting his gloves with military precision. "The weather holds. I suggest we take advantage while we may."

"Where is Merry?" Mr. Fielding asked suddenly, glancing toward the staircase. "She is usually the first to come when there is a chance of sport."

Mr. Roxton, already donning his heavy coat, sighed with an indulgent smile. "She has gone to check the lambs, I am told. Foolish girl—she thinks no creature in the county can manage without her. I dare say she will have them all named before the day is out."

The men laughed good-naturedly, but Joshua's heart tightened.

She would find peace there if anywhere—among the quiet,

trusting animals that required nothing from her but gentleness. They would comfort her when no words could.

Lennox clapped him on the shoulder. "You are brooding, Captain. Come, we will shake the melancholy from you with a good march and worse aim."

Joshua let them herd him out, the weight of the gun familiar in his hands. The cold bit cleanly through his coat as they crossed the park, several dogs bounding ahead, their eager barks scattering the morning stillness.

"Tell me truly," Simon said as they walked, "is it not absurd that Bruton still insists upon parading about that peacock, Tremaine? I should sooner trust a fox with a hen-house."

"Careful," James chided. "You will wound his pride if he ever hears you call him that. A man so devoted to mirrors might die of the shock."

Their father gave a low chuckle. "Gentlemen, you are forgetting yourselves. We are guests in this county, not barrack-room cynics. If the man is a fool, the world will discover it soon enough without our help."

Joshua's lips curved cynically. He suspected the world knew. Yet he thought of Merry, and the look in her eyes that morning—a look that had glimpsed truth and would rather not have done so.

The dogs flushed the first pheasant, and the report of a gun shattered the silence. The smell of powder mingled with wet earth and old leaves. The brothers began to call and laugh, their voices echoing down the slope. Joshua loaded and fired when his turn came, but his mind was elsewhere.

He thought of Merry's small figure, in her wool cloak, against the grey fields with the wind tugging at her hair. He thought of her crouched beside a newborn lamb and the way her voice softened when she soothed a frightened creature. Perhaps she was there now, her hands warming the tiny body, her breath mingling with the animal's as she whispered some nonsense word of comfort.

He hoped she had found peace there—that the quiet steadiness of the place would ease the jagged edges of her disappointment.

The men tramped further afield, their laughter rising again as another brace went down. Joshua reloaded methodically, his thoughts turning inward once more.

There were kinds of battles he knew how to fight: visible enemies, tangible threats, problems that could be solved with action, but the one before him now required another sort of strength. He could only wait.

He took aim again and fired, the echo rolling across the hills. A pheasant dropped, feathers scattering like confetti against the snow.

"Capital shot!" Mr. Roxton called. "That will do nicely for dinner!"

Joshua smiled faintly and lowered the gun. The smell of burnt powder drifted on the wind.

By the time they turned back toward Wychwood, the sky was heavy with unfallen snow. The others were jovial, trading boasts and laughter, but Joshua's mind lingered still on Merry, her courage unbowed though her heart was bruised.

"May she find her peace," he murmured under his breath.

"What was that?" Caleb asked, looking over.

"Nothing," Joshua said with a faint smile. "Only thinking about our dinner." And Merry.

THERE WAS no peace to be had at Wychwood, Merry discovered. Not in the hum of the passages, not in the bright chatter of the nursery, not in the murmuring of card tables or the cheerful tyranny of the drawing room fire. Everywhere she turned, the house seemed too full of noise, too bright with laughter that mocked her own thoughts. Even the tick of the great clock above the stair had become an accusation, counting each foolish moment she had wasted on a man who had never deserved her regard.

She fled into the side garden, pretending that she only wished to breathe the air. The yews stood solemnly, collecting the thin snow upon their dark boughs. Smoke drifted from the chimneys, and the air smelled of damp earth and frost. Merry stood beside the sundial—

useless in a winter noon—and told herself that in five minutes she would feel composed. The five minutes came and went, however, and her heart continued its painful rebellion—though was it her heart or her pride that was wounded? There were no answers to be found when the wound was so fresh.

At last, she went to find her mother.

Mrs. Roxton was sitting in the morning room with Mrs. Fielding, both of them industriously engaged in not doing very much at all. A basket of mending lay untouched between them, for the conversation was of neighbours and not of stockings. The moment Merry entered, her mother's eyes lifted in instinctive welcome.

"My dear," she said, noting the cast of her daughter's cheeks, "you have been out without your proper hat again."

"I am going home," Merry said steadily. "Roxton House is quieter, and I wish to look in on the lambs."

Her mother gave her a long, measuring look—one that saw far more than Merry intended to show—and nodded. "You may go, if you promise to dine with us tonight. Your father will send for you himself if you are late."

Mrs. Fielding nodded approval. Clearly, they had heard the gossip.

Merry curtsied, kissed their cheeks, and escaped before either could offer more sympathy. Within half an hour, a groom had been called, her mare saddled, and she was riding through the pale winter lanes toward home.

The road between Wychwood and the Roxton estate wound through frost-edged fields, the hedgerows bare but sparkling in the thin light. The sky promised more snow before evening. Merry rode swiftly, welcoming the sharp air against her face. When she reached her own gate, the familiar sight of the home farm steadied her—its smaller, plainer windows, the honest smoke from the chimney, the low murmur of ewes in the fold.

Dawkins appeared at the pen with his habitual grave smile.

"You be early for the New Year, Miss Merry," he said. "Two ewes have lambed, and another's thinking of it. I'd wager she is but waiting to make certain we be watching."

Merry dismounted and passed him the reins. "I am come to reason with her, then. No creature in Gloucestershire has yet held out against me."

Dawkins chuckled and led her toward the lambing pens. The warm musky scent of straw and lamb enveloped her the instant she stepped inside the old barn. The ewes murmured softly, their great dark eyes shining in the lamplight. There was a peace here—earthy, practical, forgiving—that soothed her as nothing else could. The animals cared not that she had been betrayed and would never be a fine lady.

"That one is struggling to suckle," Dawkins remarked.

Without being told, Merry began to help. She knelt beside the smallest ewe, coaxing the feeble lamb to drink, her hands firm and practised. The tiny creature fumbled at first, then found its strength and began to suckle greedily. Merry's shoulders relaxed. For the first time all morning, she was able to smile.

"There, now," she murmured. "You see? You only needed patience and persuasion."

When the lamb had finished, she settled against the timber wall, cradling the warm bundle in her lap. The steadiness of its heartbeat against her arm was an answer to something she had not dared to voice. And yet, even here, the ache remained.

She could no longer deny what must be done.

Setting the lamb carefully in the straw, she rose, brushed the straw from her skirt, crossed to the house and went into the small parlour to write. The pen was blunt, the ink cold, but her hand was steady as she wrote:

Sir,

You asked me to keep a secret. I will not. I cannot be engaged to a man who will not acknowledge me in daylight, who gives one name to me and another to the world. You have been lavish with words, but I require honour, not eloquence. There is to be no betrothal, secret or otherwise. You will not call upon my father. You will not call upon me. Seek your fortune where you and your father have chosen. I wish you as much honesty as you can find, and as much kindness as you can learn.

MR

SHE READ IT ONCE, sealed it and directed it. Dawkins sent young Tom to deliver it to the Crown with instructions to forward it to Lord Bruton's house. Tom, wise enough not to ask questions, rode off at once with the air of a boy entrusted with state secrets.

The letter gone, Merry returned to the sheep. There was always more work—water to draw, straw to turn, lamps to trim. She lost herself in it gladly, but as the hours passed and the sky turned pearly grey, the first measure of peace she had gained began to slip away. She knew she must return.

The lamb she had been tending stirred in the straw beside her. She took up the bottle once more and settled against the wall to feed it. The little creature's trust was complete and unthinking, which made her own shame all the sharper.

"How wise you are," she whispered. "You want only warmth and food and company. You do not mistake pretty words for goodness."

Footsteps sounded on the stone outside. She assumed it was Dawkins until Joshua Fielding stood in the lamplight before her.

He had hung his hat on a nail; damp hair clung to his temples. He looked, as ever, too tall for comfort and too composed for pity.

"Miss Roxton," he said quietly. "Your mother has asked me to fetch you home—if you wished to come."

Merry blinked at him, uncertain whether to laugh or cry. "That sounds precisely like her," she said.

Joshua smiled faintly. "It does."

He came no nearer, which was kind of him. The lamb stirred, and Merry resumed feeding it. He watched in silence, his hands in his coat pockets. There was something profoundly steady in his presence; even the animals seemed to sense it.

"I passed Tom on the road," he said after a while. "He had a letter—and a look that suggested I ought not to ask what was in it."

Merry nodded. "Then you know."

He inclined his head, not pressing her.

"I have let Mr. Tremaine know," she said at last. "There will be no more courting." Merry hesitated. How she wished she could tell him that Tremaine had proposed, but that would only increase her shame.

His eyes met hers with quiet understanding. "You did rightly."

She wanted to thank him, but the words tangled themselves and would not be said. It was far too easy to speak honestly with him. "I suppose it ought to make me feel better," she said, "but it does not. I thought myself shrewd enough to judge a man's worth. I was wrong."

Joshua shook his head. "You were not wrong to believe in goodness. You were wrong only to believe it might be found in him."

Merry looked down at the lamb, blinking hard. "It is humiliating, all the same. I prided myself on not being the sort of girl to be taken in by a handsome face. I even pitied those who were."

He crouched beside her then, resting one arm on his knee. "You are not the first to be deceived by a charming rogue, and you will not be the last. I have seen officers gamble away their fortunes for a horse with a glossy coat and bad legs. There is no shame in mistaking surface for substance when the polish is well done."

Despite herself, she laughed. The lamb finished drinking and nosed sleepily against Joshua's sleeve. Merry smiled in spite of herself. "You see? Even this little creature trusts you."

"She is an excellent judge of character," he said gravely.

They laughed softly together, and the warmth between them was not only that of the lamplight.

When she had composed herself, she said, "Tell me truthfully, Captain—did you already know?"

He hesitated only a moment. "My superior wrote to me. He knows Lord Bruton. The family has brought a young lady down from London—a Miss Dunning, daughter to a wealthy man. Her father hesitates over the match because of Tremaine's debts and reputation but Bruton is determined upon it."

"So," Merry said quietly, "the gossip was true."

"It was," Joshua said. "His debts are…considerable."

She nodded, absorbing it without flinching. "Then I was only ever a convenience. A country diversion while he waited for better prospects."

Joshua's expression softened. "You were never a convenience. The pressure from his father is considerable."

Her throat ached. "You are too generous."

"Only honest," he said simply.

The wind whistled faintly through the chinks in the boards. The lamb wriggled between them, warm and alive.

When she finally rose, Joshua offered his hand—not in gallantry, but as a steadying presence. She took it.

"Will you come to Wychwood?" he asked.

"Yes," she said, after a pause. "I have done what I must here."

By the time they reached Wychwood, dusk had thickened into early night. The windows shone golden through the mist, and warmth met them before they crossed the threshold. Mrs. Roxton received her daughter without question, merely a kiss upon her forehead.

The household was in lively disorder, preparing for the New Year's Eve celebration. Unlike many households, the children were to be allowed up past their usual bedtime. Thrilled, they ran in and out of the hall, paper crowns askew, clutching wooden trumpets that produced more enthusiasm than tune. The grown-ups pretended not to mind.

As was tradition, the families gathered around the great hearth. Cheese toast was made on long forks, the gentlemen declaring themselves experts while the women exchanged amused glances. The children sang nursery rhymes far too loudly and forgot half the words. Laughter filled the house, softening even the ache in Merry's chest.

Joshua sat near the fire, helping Roger—his arm still bound from the mishap skating—to turn the fork without spilling the toast into the fire. Merry watched him for a long moment, struck by how easily he fit among them, how naturally the children leaned toward him, how quietly he seemed to belong.

When midnight neared, the room hushed. The clock's slow toll filled the silence, and as the final stroke faded, a cheer rose up—ragged, joyful, human. Glasses clinked.

"To health!" cried Mr. Roxton.

"To prosperity!" said Mr. Fielding.

"To happiness," added Mrs. Fielding softly.

"And to kindness," said Mrs. Roxton, her eyes on her daughter.

Merry raised her glass but said nothing. *To courage,* she thought, but she kept the word to herself.

When she looked up, Joshua's eyes were on her. He smiled—quietly, without presumption—and inclined his head.

"May the new year bring you joy, Miss Roxton," he said.

"Likewise, Captain Fielding," she answered.

And though the ache in her heart was not gone, something in her steadied. She had faced what she must. She had chosen honesty over illusion—and perhaps, she thought, as laughter rose again around them, courage was its own beginning.

CHAPTER 12

New Year's Day. Joshua was not one for resolutions, but he felt a little lighter in his heart, a bit more hopeful now that Merry had decided to break with Tremaine, and she had seen the man's perfidy for herself with minimal interference from Joshua.

By noon, the ladies had bundled themselves into shawls and pelisses, and were heading down the lane in the carriage to call upon Mrs. Hargreaves and her new baby. Blankets, little caps, and lace-trimmed, woollen bootees filled their baskets. The gentlemen turned toward the village instead. Someone had declared they should join the annual village skittles tournament in honour of the year's turning, and that it would be a shame to offend tradition.

The tavern was already thick with warmth when they entered, their boots stamping snow on to the flags. A smell of oak smoke, ale, and roasted onions wrapped the room like a familiar coat. The landlord's broad grin greeted them before his words did.

"Ah, my fine gentlemen! The barn is prepared, and there are prizes that will make a man proud of his eyesight!"

"Prizes?" Mr. Roxton echoed. "You mean a pint for whoever misses least and infamy for whoever misses most?"

The villagers laughed, and everyone began with a pint. Before long, Joshua found himself in the barn next door, standing holding the bowl, the hum of good spirits about him. Chalk dusted the air as the steward kept score, and the small crowd cheered every knocked-down pin as if it mattered to the Empire.

"Steady, Captain," Mr. Roxton called as he carried a tray with tankards of ale in from the tavern. "No military precision, if you please—let the rest of us have a chance!"

Joshua grinned, threw, and hit the pins cleanly. The company answered with a low, approving murmur.

It was just then that Barnaby Tremaine arrived.

The door swung wide; a gust of cold air curled through the room. He came in, his attire too polished for the company—coat of bottle green, neckcloth stiff enough to hang a hat on. His colour was high, his smile careless, and the smell of gin clung faintly beneath his cologne.

Tremaine's voice carried above the talk. "Gentlemen! I could hear the laughter from halfway through the village. What game has you all in such good humour?"

"Skittles," Caleb answered. "Would you care to join us?"

"With pleasure," he returned, sweeping off his gloves. "But I could not insult such excellent players without adding some interest to the matter. What is a game without a wager?"

Joshua paused with his wooden bowl in mid-aim. "A friendly game remains friendly, Mr. Tremaine."

Tremaine smiled; there were too many teeth in it. "Friendship without stakes is a dull business, Captain. A sovereign says I can best you in three rounds."

A hush fell. Men who had been laughing a moment ago suddenly studied their tankards. There was no refusing without the landlord's interference, and he would not nay-say the lord's son.

Joshua's voice stayed mild. "Very well—one sovereign." He laid the coin down flat on a table beside the alley. "No more."

The match began. Tremaine's first toss knocked over several pins; the next, he hit the centre. He turned with a flourish, one hand out for applause that never came. Joshua followed, hitting all but the centre pin at once. The third round ended with a rout by Joshua knocking down all at once, and the crowd's good humour returned in a rush of clapping and talk.

But Tremaine wasn't content with that. In a louder voice than necessary, he ordered another round of gin. His laugh grew sharper, his gestures broader. Before long, he was flinging coins on the table at every new opponent, his voice slurred just enough to draw sidelong looks.

Two men unknown to Joshua entered, rougher in dress and manner, and took a corner without ordering. Their eyes swept around the barn once, then stayed on Tremaine.

Joshua noted them without seeming to. Men like that did not come to admire a village skittles tournament. Had they, perhaps, followed Tremaine?

The two men did not drink. Their silence weighed heavier than the talk. One of them—a wiry fellow with a narrow face and eyes like steel pins—took out a pocket ledger, turned a page, and tapped his pencil once. Joshua caught the motion and understood.

The first blow came after the last round of throws. Tremaine lost badly, cursed the pins, and demanded another go. When no one would answer, the tournament carried on. With a furious glare at the assembled, Tremaine walked into the tap-room and demanded more drink. Surreptitiously, the two men followed him into the inn, crossing the room with unhurried purpose. Trailing in their wake, Joshua sidled close enough to listen.

"Mr. Tremaine," the taller one said. His voice had the edge of London in it. "A word with you, if you please."

Tremaine gave a laugh that had lost its shine. "My dear fellow, can it not wait? You will spoil the sport."

"It has waited long enough."

The shorter man jerked his chin toward the back door. The landlord, wiping a pewter mug, looked down and said nothing.

Tremaine hesitated, saw the eyes on him, and straightened his shoulders. "Of course. A private matter. Excuse me, gentlemen."

Joshua watched them leave, then he moved after them, as silent as a shadow.

The yard behind the Crown was half frozen mud, half puddle, the air sharp with smoke from the kitchen chimney. A cat streaked away as the door creaked open.

Tremaine stood between the men now, still playing at bravado. "I shall have funds within the week."

"A week?" the shorter man said, his voice a rasp of mockery. "You are lucky the master gave you till New Year's Eve. You 'ave stretched that, too."

"I have a new arrangement in hand. A betrothal to an heiress."

The taller man shifted his stance. "Is that so? We know Dunning left and took 'is daughter with 'im. 'E 'ad you looked into. 'E did not like what 'e found. Called you—what was it, Ned?"

The other man spat into the snow. "A worthless wastrel, sir, and that were the kindest bit. Said if 'e lent you a guinea, 'e wud want the watch off your wrist as proof you couldn't wager it first."

Tremaine's face drained.

"We watched 'is carriage roll out this mornin'." The shorter man's boot prodded a patch of ice. "You'd best find another 'eiress to mend your fortunes, an' quick." He laughed.

Joshua could see Tremaine's mind considering his options, and he knew before the man spoke what he would say.

"Dunning was my father's choice!" Tremaine's voice cracked. "I have a betrothed—Roxton's daughter. It only wants a license. Allow me three days and she will be my wife."

The two men exchanged wary glances.

"I assure you!" Tremaine pleaded.

"What do you think, Marv? Is 'e tellin' the truth?"

The next sound was the thud of a fist. Tremaine folded against the wall, gasping.

"Mebbe. Mebbe not." Another brutal fist met Tremaine's eye then another split his lip.

The taller man gave a dry chuckle, half contempt, half scorn. "See you marry this 'eiress. You 'ave three days, no more. Fail, and you'll be wishing for my fist instead of what waits fer you."

The second man gave him a parting kick, precise and merciless, before turning away.

"Three days, and we will be watchin,'" the Cockney said again, his grin all rotten teeth. "We ain't the sort to count to four."

They vanished into the lane as quietly as they had come.

Joshua stepped forward. Tremaine was hunched by the barrels, hands pressed to his ribs, breath coming in sharp, shallow gasps. When he looked up, his eyes flared with resentment rather than shame.

"Fielding," he spat. "Here to congratulate yourself?"

Joshua bent, caught him by the arm, and pulled him upright. "Save your pride. The ground's cold."

"Go to the devil."

"After you." Joshua steadied him until he could stand.

Back inside the tavern, clatter of tongues had resumed—and the business of men pretending not to have seen what they had. Joshua guided Tremaine to the table and poured a mug of water, setting it before him.

The man's hand trembled as he drank. He wiped his mouth with the back of his glove and leaned closer. "Were you eavesdropping?"

Joshua did not answer.

"She will have me yet," Tremaine muttered. "She has promised. Her word is given."

"Her word," Joshua said, low enough that only Tremaine could hear, "was taken by deceit. It is not binding."

Tremaine's smile twisted. "We will see about that, Fielding."

He pushed to his feet and swayed, half-defiant yet half-broken. A few of the villagers moved aside to make way for him. He threw down a coin, sneered at its smallness, and stalked toward the door.

Joshua let him go. Outside, the wind was swirling and harsh. The men of Wychwood and Roxton followed him, boots crunching the snow that had already begun to gather in the ruts.

"What happened?" Matthew asked.

Joshua adjusted his gloves. "He is in trouble with moneylenders. They gave him three days' grace."

Mr. Roxton frowned. "And that concerns us?"

"It does," Joshua said. "He is desperate…and desperate men chase whatever they think might save them."

The older man's face hardened. "Merry."

Joshua nodded once. "We must keep her close. He is badly dipped."

They said no more after that. The wind rose, driving the snow in thin white ribbons along the hedgerows. When the house lights came into view. Joshua's stride lengthened. He had no intention of ever again letting Barnaby Tremaine come within a hundred yards of Merry.

THE VISIT to Mrs. Hargreaves ought to have been a cheerful one. The ladies had filled the cottage with laughter and admiration, their arms laden with blankets and gowns, their voices softening instinctively in the presence of the new baby.

Merry had smiled and admired like the rest, but when the infant's tiny fingers closed around hers, something inside her wavered. The soft warmth, the sweet milky scent, the absolute trust of the little creature—all stirred a melancholy she could neither name nor control.

It was ridiculous, she told herself as she rode back in the Fieldings' carriage. Ridiculous and ungrateful, she told herself irritably. She had her health, her family and more than enough comfort. Yet the image would not leave her: the baby's cheek nestled against its mother's neck, the quiet contentment of belonging.

By the time the carriage turned away from the village, she could bear the confinement of it no longer.

"Would you mind setting me down at the home farm?" she asked. "I should like to see how the lambs are doing. Dawkins can bring me home later."

Her mother gave her a knowing look but nodded, and Mrs.

Fielding relayed her instructions to the coachman, who, used to the whims of his betters, said nothing. When the carriage halted before the familiar low buildings, Merry stepped down into the crisp afternoon and the carriage rolled on. The sky hung white and thin, the air sharp enough to make her breath cloud. The bleating of ewes came faintly from the fold.

Dawkins emerged from the barn wiping his hands on a bit of sacking. His grey hair stuck out beneath his cap, and his ruddy face brightened when he saw her.

"Good day to you, Miss Merry. I had not expected you again so soon."

"I wished to see the new lambs," she said, smiling a little. "I thought the fresh air might cure my restlessness."

He chuckled. "Ah, the country's physic, that is. I was just about to step up to the house for my dinner. My daughter's roastin' a goose, and if I don't appear soon, she will send the boy to fetch me by the ear."

Merry shook her head. "Do not stay on my account. I want only to spend a little time among them. I will be quite safe here."

Dawkins hesitated, looking toward the darkening edge of the fields. "Very well, miss. I will not be long. I shall fetch you back to Wychwood myself."

"Do not rush," she said kindly. "I promise not to lose my way between one pen and the next."

He tipped his cap and went off down the lane, whistling.

Merry turned toward the lambing sheds. The familiar smell of straw and barn rose about her like a balm. She could hear the soft rustle of animals settling, the rhythmic thud of a ewe pawing the bedding. The smallest of the lambs—the one she had fed with the bottle—tottered toward her and butted its head against her knee. She bent to stroke its woolly back and smiled.

"Ah, little one," she murmured. "You have more sense than most people I know."

The familiar calmed her at once. She moved through the pens, righting a tipped pail here, smoothing a fleece there, speaking softly to each creature as she passed. The wind moaned faintly through the eaves, carrying the smell of snow.

She was bending to check a lamb when a shadow moved across the doorway.

"Merry."

She straightened, her hand gripping the top rail. Barnaby Tremaine stood there, the low light behind him, his coat askew and his cravat undone. He looked as if he had not slept in a day—or a week. The pallor of his face was startling against the red of his eyes.

"Mr. Tremaine?" Her heart gave a quick, frightened leap. "What are you doing here?"

"I came to see you." His smile was uneven. "You have been avoiding me."

"I wrote to you," she said, fighting to keep her voice even. "There was nothing left to say."

He stepped inside, and the smell of spirits came with him, pungent and unmistakable. "Ah, yes, the letter. A trifle dramatic, do you not think?"

"It was simply the truth."

His eyes flickered, and for a moment she thought she saw shame— but it passed too quickly. "How did you know I would be here?" she asked.

"As it happens," he said, "I saw your carriage from the village. I followed."

Her pulse quickened. "You followed me?"

"Do not look so alarmed. You left me no choice." He took another step forward. The slush on his boots darkened the straw. "You will not listen to reason otherwise. We belong together, Merry. You know it as well as I."

She moved a pace back, her heel brushing the side of a trough. "You are mistaken. You must leave now."

He reached for her arm, but she jerked away. His fingers caught the edge of her sleeve. "Please, Barnaby. You have had too much to drink. You are not yourself."

"I am more myself than ever!" he burst out. "Your family has poisoned you against me, that sanctimonious Fielding especially. Do you think he cares for you? He only wants to ruin me."

"I want nothing to do with any of this," she said, her voice shaking. "Let me go."

He drew a breath, his expression changing from pleading to determination. "You are making me do this, Merry. It should not have been this way."

"What do you mean?"

Before she could move, he seized her wrist. She struggled, but his grip tightened painfully. "Barnaby, stop this!"

"Listen to me!" he hissed, dragging her closer. "If you come with me now—tonight—we can be married within days. Once you are my wife, they can do nothing to part us."

"Let me go!" she cried, wrenching against him. The lambs bleated nervously, one knocking over a pail that clattered on the earthen floor.

He pressed her back against the wall. The wild look in his eyes chilled her more than the cold. "I need you, Merry," he said hoarsely. "Do not make me force what should be given willingly."

Her heart thudded in terror. "You cannot mean to—?"

But he was already drawing a length of rope from his coat and before she could twist away, he caught both her wrists. The rough hemp scraped her skin as he bound her hands before her.

"Barnaby! Please—this is madness!"

"It must be done."

He pulled her out into the yard. The pale light was dimming fast. His horse waited near the fence, stamping impatiently, its flanks lathered as though it had been ridden hard. He threw her over the saddle like a sack of potatoes.

"Stop!" she cried. "You will regret this!"

Her words were swallowed by the wind. Tremaine mounted behind her, his arm clamping around her, trying to force her upright. The rope cut into her wrists as she struggled. He jerked the reins, and the horse lurched and then plunged forward down the lane.

Cold air lashed her face. The trees blurred. She could hear nothing but the pounding of hooves and the rasp of his breath close to her ear.

"Barnaby, please," she gasped. "This will ruin us both!"

"Better ruin than to lose you," he shouted over the wind. "They will understand when we are wed."

She twisted, trying to throw herself free, but his grip was iron-hard. The rope bit deeper. Panic rose sharp and blinding—if she fell now, she might break her neck.

"No!" she cried once, the sound lost to the empty fields.

The lane curved and branches whipped at her cloak. The village lights were a distant smear of gold far behind them. Dawkins would not return for an hour at least. Who would think to look for her before nightfall?

Her mind raced uselessly, searching for anything that might save her—a rider on the road, a gate left open, the mercy of a startled horse. The only answer was the wind and the cruel rhythm of the gallop.

The last thing she saw before darkness swallowed the fields was the flicker of Wychwood's chimneys through the trees—warm and safe but impossibly far away.

CHAPTER 13

The cold wind had seeped deep into his bones by the time Joshua and the other men reached Wychwood. Their boots tracked melting snow across the flagged floor as they shrugged out of their coats, laughter fading when they saw Mrs. Roxton standing by the hearth, her face tight with unease.

"Where is Merry?" Mr. Roxton asked, his brow furrowing as he glanced around the hall.

"She went to the home farm after visiting Mrs. Hargreaves," Mrs. Roxton said. "Dawkins was to bring her back. I thought she would be here by now."

Mr. Lennox was already reaching for his gloves again. "Then we will ride there and fetch her. The roads are turning slick. She ought not be out after dark."

Roxton turned to the butler. "Have the grooms saddle fresh horses and light lanterns. Lennox, you and I will take the lower road to the home farm. Fielding—stay here, will you? She may have come another way."

Joshua hesitated only a moment before following them to the stables. Nevertheless, even as he tightened the girth on one of the horses, he forced himself to think. Panic never served anyone.

The men moved quickly, the sound of hooves and harness echoing in the bitter air.

Joshua knew Merry—she would have stayed near the lambs, perhaps lost in thought, but she would not have ventured back alone on foot. There was no reason to assume danger yet.

The odds were slim of Tremaine looking for her there. He would know she was spending Christmas-tide at Wychwood, surrounded by family and servants. Even a desperate man would hesitate to strike when she was surrounded.

Roxton and Lennox would bring her back within the hour, he told himself. He would laugh about his worry later. And when Tremaine's debts came due, his troubles would end one way or another, either by his father's intervention or that of the money-lenders.

Joshua stayed near the front steps, pacing up and down while listening for hoof beats. The minutes stretched. The snow fell harder, muffling all sound. He glanced at the great clock in the hall as the hands crawled toward eight.

Then, at last, horses clattered up the drive. However, when Mr. Roxton and Mr. Lennox dismounted, their faces were grave.

"She is not there," Roxton said. His voice, usually a deep and jovial rumble, was as tight as a bowstring. "Dawkins met us on the lane in a near-frantic state. He said he returned to find the shed in disarray—a pail overturned, straw scattered, and one of the pens unfastened. There were tracks. It looked as though a horse had bolted—or been ridden off in a hurry."

Joshua's stomach dropped, though he kept his expression steady. "There was no sign of her?"

"None. Only her cloak. Dawkins said it was lying by the door."

Mrs. Roxton gave a cry and pressed her hand to her mouth. The room erupted in confusion—orders, half-formed plans, the scraping of chairs. Joshua moved to the window, staring into the snow as if he could force it to give up its secrets.

"Dawkins was gone less than an hour. She told him to go home to his family, bless her," Mr. Roxton explained.

The room grew very quiet. The only sound was the hiss of the fire and the distant ticking of the long-case clock.

"She would not have gone off of her own accord," Mrs. Roxton said faintly. "Not without sending word."

"Not in this weather," Joshua said, more to himself than anyone else.

The great doors opened again, and cold air rushed in. A tall figure stepped inside, wrapped in a dark travelling cloak powdered with snow. The butler's voice rang out: "Lord Bruton, my lord."

Every head turned.

Bruton—the lines at his eyes deepened by worry—paused on the threshold and inclined his head. "Forgive this intrusion. I fear I may be the bearer of bad news—or at least of bad suspicions."

Roxton strode forward. "You have seen your son?"

"Not since this morning." Bruton's expression was grim. "But I was told what happened at the tavern. My man was there and followed the moneylenders when they left, fearing Barnaby would do something rash. When the Dunnings left for London today, Barnaby was furious. He said he had spoken of a marriage, of securing himself before his debts were called. He reported that your daughter's name had been on Barnaby's lips." He shook his head. "I should never have let it go this far."

Mrs. Roxton swayed; Lennox caught her arm. "You believe he has taken her?" she whispered.

Bruton's jaw clenched. "It appears I am too late to prevent it. How may I help?"

Roxton drew a slow breath, steadying himself. "We must divide our efforts. If he means to marry her by force, there are two possibilities—north for Gretna Green, or south for London."

Bruton spoke, his voice firm. "I doubt he will risk Scotland. It is too far in this storm, and he lacks the funds.

Joshua spoke. "If he is riding for a special license, London is his best chance."

Bruton nodded. "My thoughts exactly. My credit will carry him that far, and he has lodgings there."

"Then we follow that trail," Joshua said. "If we are wrong, the others will find him travelling north."

"Agreed." Roxton turned to the others. "Lennox, Caleb, Simon—take the road through Gloucester and northward. If he has fled that way, intercept him before the border."

The men nodded, already striding for the door. The hall filled with the sharp scent of cold air, as unwelcoming as the task ahead. The hall erupted in motion. Servants hurried in every direction—boots clattering, doors slamming, the smell of wet leather and lamp oil filling the air. Joshua moved among them, giving quiet instructions, checking pistols and flints, ensuring each man carried coin and cloak enough. He could feel the house's tension thrumming like a vessel about to burst.

Joshua turned to Bruton. "We shall need fast horses and no delay. If we ride through the night, we can reach London by tomorrow evening."

Bruton's face was pale, but his eyes were clear. "I have my horse. "Might I join you?"

Mrs. Roxton clutched her husband's sleeve. "Bring her back to me. Bring my daughter home."

He kissed her hand, his own voice roughened. "We will, my dear, come what may."

Joshua followed Bruton out into the snow. The wind bit hard now, the flakes stinging his face as the horses were brought around. He swung into the saddle, glancing once toward the dark shape of the house—toward the windows that glowed faintly through the storm. Somewhere beyond those hills, Merry was in the hands of a man who was beyond reason.

Bruton mounted beside him, the lines of worry in his face deepening under the lantern light. "He is my son," he said quietly, "but if he has harmed her—"

Joshua looked straight ahead. "He will not. We will find him first."

They spurred their horses and rode into the storm. The snow swallowed the sound of hooves, and the night closed behind them like a curtain.

The storm clawed at Joshua's cloak as they rode, and the world shrank to the circle of lantern light between his horse's ears. He had known cold before—barracks in Flanders, marches through sleet—but this was different. Then, he had thought only of survival. Now, every gust whispered Merry's name, every shadow looked like danger.

He could not stop thinking of her—the last time he had seen her, smiling faintly over her glass as they had toasted the new year's birth. He had meant to speak with her that evening, to say something half-formed but necessary. Now, those unsaid words burned like coals in his chest.

When they paused at the crossroads to fix a slipping girth, Bruton muttered a curse that vanished into the snow. Joshua barely heard him. His thoughts had gone elsewhere—into the black possibilities that lay between one mile and the next. What if she had fallen? What if she was hurt? The image of her cloak lying in the straw would not leave him. He had seen a thousand battlefields and yet none had turned his stomach quite like that single thought: Merry, frightened, frozen, and alone.

He tightened his reins and pressed Brutus onward. Beneath the snow, the horse's breath steamed like smoke, strong and steady. Joshua bent low over the saddle, eyes narrowed against the flurries. He was not a man given to fear, but now fear had shape and name. It was not for his own life—it was for hers.

He remembered her courage—how she had faced the villagers' gossip with composure, how she had tended the lambs with patience even in the cold. She was not the kind of woman to yield easily. That thought steadied him.

If she could see him now, he wondered, would she know what she meant to him? Would she understand that this inner fire was not born of duty or friendship, but of something far more dangerous and dear?

He no longer tried to deny his feelings for her. It came to him as plainly as breath in his lungs. He had crossed countries for his king, faced cannon fire without trembling—but the thought of what might happen to her, stripped him bare.

When Bruton called a halt to check their bearings, Joshua turned his face upward into the snow. The flakes struck cold, but they hissed to nothing against the heat of that new, consuming truth.

He would find her. Whatever it cost, whatever road it took, he would find her.

For the first time in his life, war seemed easier than peace—because in war, at least, you knew the enemy. Here, the foe was distance, and darkness, and the unthinkable possibility of arriving too late.

He gritted his teeth and set his heels to his horse's sides. The storm swallowed him whole, but he did not falter. Somewhere ahead, Merry waited, and he would not stop until she was safe in his arms again.

THE WORLD HAD BECOME a blur of snow and motion. The horse's hooves struck hard and fast against the frozen road, throwing up clods of ice. The wind tore at Merry's skirts, and the raw rope cut deep into her wrists. She had long since stopped feeling her fingers; they hung useless and frozen by the icy chill.

Her body ached from the awkward way she was pinned against Tremaine, every jolt of the saddle sending pain through her spine. She was not dressed for riding—not in thin half-boots and a gown better suited for morning calls than gallops through winter fields. Her bonnet had flown off miles ago. Her hair, loosened by the wind, streamed against her face like a whip.

The horse stumbled once. The poor beast was breathing hard, its coat dark with sweat despite the cold. "Barnaby, for pity's sake!" she cried, her voice hoarse from the cold air. "You will kill us and the horse if you keep this pace!"

He said nothing at first, his jaw clenched and his hands white on the reins. Then, with a curse, he pulled up sharply. Trembling, the animal stopped in a storm of snow.

"Very well," he said, panting. "We should have enough of a start to stop—but not for long, mind you."

Merry sagged in the saddle, her legs shaking with relief. She could barely feel them. The cold had gone beyond biting—it had become dull and steady, the kind that crept inward. She flexed her hands, trying to bring back sensation.

Barnaby turned in the saddle to scan the road behind them. The pale fields stretched on forever, empty and still. "No one yet," he muttered. "Good."

Merry wanted to speak, to reason with him, but her voice came out faint. "Where are you taking me?"

He glanced down at her, a flash of impatience in his eyes. "You know perfectly well. To be married. Where else?"

"I thought—" She swallowed hard. "I thought you meant Gretna Green."

He gave a short, unpleasant laugh. "A fool's journey, that. Scotland is several days' hard ride, and I've no wish to freeze my bones on the road. London will do. There are parsons enough there willing to overlook the niceties."

London. The word struck her like a blow. London meant hiding places, crowds, and her family's pursuit delayed by distance.

Her mind raced even as her limbs refused to move. She must delay him—somehow, any way she could.

The horse shifted uneasily, blowing steam from its nostrils. Merry touched her lips to speak again, but the sound that came out was little more than a whisper. "I am frozen."

"You will survive," he said shortly, swinging down to the ground. "We will change to a carriage. You can warm yourself then."

She nearly slid from the saddle, her body too stiff to obey her. When her feet touched the ground, they buckled. Tremaine caught her by the arm—not gently—and half dragged her toward a low-roofed inn where light flickered through shuttered windows. She could see little else around, and had no idea where she was. He untied the ropes with a warning. "Do not try anything or I will tie your feet as well."

Inside, warmth hit her like a slap, painful after the frost. The landlord hurried forward, blinking at the sight of her tangled hair and pale face. Tremaine's look was enough to silence any question. "A private carriage," he said, tossing down coins. "Now. Hitched and ready within the quarter-hour."

The landlord bowed and disappeared. Merry stood swaying, numb from cold and fear, her mind working furiously.

"Sit down," Tremaine ordered, gesturing toward a chair by the fire. "You look ready to swoon."

She obeyed, more from weakness than compliance. The heat stung her frozen fingers until she nearly cried out. She rubbed them together, hiding the returning pain behind her sleeve.

"I told you that you had no business defying me."

"I did not defy you," she managed to say, looking up at him. "I refused you. That is not the same thing."

His eyes darkened, but before he could speak, the landlord returned. "The carriage is ready, sir."

Tremaine nodded curtly.

Merry tried one last approach. "I need something warm," she said faintly, "and perhaps—perhaps I could rest a moment longer?"

He studied her for a beat, then smiled thinly. "You miss the mark, my love. You are as cunning as a fox, but I know every trick you might play." He seized her wrist again. "Come."

She flinched at his touch, but he only tightened his grip, steering her through along the passage and out into the yard where the carriage waited, dark and square against the snow. The driver sat hunched on the box, muffled to the chin.

The moment she stepped inside, she knew escape would be near impossible. There was little space to manouevre, and the single lamp threw light over the front seat only. Tremaine followed, slammed the door, pulled out a flask and drank heavily. The night only wanted him heavy with drink.

"Now," he said, tucking the flask inside his coat before beginning to loop another length of rope through the door handle and around her wrists. "No foolishness. I cannot have you throwing yourself out like some romantic heroine."

The humiliation burned almost hotter than the fire had. "You are making a fine mess of yourself, Barnaby," she said quietly. "You will regret this before the day is out."

He gave a bitter laugh. "I am far beyond regrets. By the time they find us, you will be my wife, and all of this will have become quite respectable."

Her throat tightened. "Is that what you told Lady Lydia, too? The lady in the sleigh? Was she part of your plan?"

He froze, then shot her a look so cold it startled her. "Watch your tongue, Merry."

She stared at him, the last fragile thread of hope fraying. "How much do you owe, Barnaby?"

He gave a short, ugly laugh. "Enough to make my name worth nothing in London. Enough that marriage is the only credit left to me." He took the flask back out and drained it.

"Then there is no hope for love at all," she said softly.

He leaned back, his eyes gleaming with something close to madness. "It is what love becomes when one is desperate. You will learn to forgive it—or not, as you choose."

And then, as if the words—or drink—had exhausted him, he shut his eyes and leaned against the seat. Within minutes, the rattling rhythm of the wheels and swaying coach deepened into a coarse snore.

Merry sat motionless, every muscle poised. The rope at her wrists rubbed raw against her skin, but she began to work at it anyway— tiny, careful movements; twisting, easing the knots loose a fraction at a time. Her heart thudded so loudly she feared it would wake him.

The carriage rocked over a rut; the jolt loosened one knot further. She felt the first trace of air on her skin as the rope slipped half an inch.

Outside, the wind howled through the trees. She could see nothing but the faint gleam of moonlight through the small window.

Another jolt—another inch. She kept her breathing shallow, every fibre intent on the slow, secret motion of her hands.

At last, the rope gave way. She sat still, scarcely daring to believe it. Tremaine stirred, muttered something incoherent, then settled again.

Merry waited for a count of ten, then twenty. Slowly, silently, she slid her hands free.

Then she got to work. Once she was satisfied that Barnaby could not easily give chase, she glanced towards the door.

It was now or never.

Merry drew a deep breath, gathered what was left of her strength, and reached for the door latch.

The cold rushed in, sharp and bright. Barnaby did not stir that time, the drink having made him insensate.

Thankfully, the pace was slow, and the jump would be softened by the snow.

She looked once at Tremaine, slumped and snoring, then eased herself forward, her pulse hammering in her ears.

"God help me," she whispered, and slipped her hands through the opening, feeling for the edge to grasp. The wind tore at her hair, but she didn't stop. Inch by inch, hanging on to the rim of the roof, she forced herself through the door and shut it behind her.

The wheels hit a rut. The carriage swayed. She took her chance, drew in one breath, and threw herself out into the snow.

The world went white, spinning around her. Then came the shock of cold, the hard slap of ground, and the roaring silence of the night.

She rolled once, twice, until a snow drift stopped her. For a moment she could not move, only lie where she was, gasping. Then she heard the carriage rolling on, unaware, the sound fading into the wind.

Merry pushed herself up onto her knees. Her cloak was gone, her hands were frozen with slush and her whole body was trembling from the fall—but she was free.

And somewhere behind her, help would be coming. She need only find safety for now.

She turned her face toward the way home and began to walk.

CHAPTER 14

The storm thickened until sight itself seemed to freeze. Joshua rode low over Brutus's neck, his eyes stinging, his every muscle taut with purpose. They had been riding for what felt like hours, following faint wheel ruts that wavered and vanished beneath each new drift. Once, they thought they'd lost the trail entirely until Bruton spotted a fresh gouge in the ditch—a mark of iron rim scraping ice. That thin sign was enough to drive them harder.

Roxton urged his horse forward, his breath coming in white plumes. "They're close!" he shouted, though the gale all but stole his voice. Joshua's heart thudded like a drumbeat of pursuit. Every gust seemed to whisper Merry's name—every shadow might have hidden her, cold and frightened.

The lamps of the cart showed first—two blurred coins wading through the snow—then the shape of the driver, hunched and black against the whitening hedges. Joshua raised a hand. Brutus checked at once, hocks under him, his breath appearing like smoke. Mr. Roxton and Lord Bruton ranged alongside, the three of them a dark line across the road.

"Ho! Coachman!" Roxton called. "Draw aside. We mean no harm."

The driver, muffled to the eyes, hunched his shoulders as if he might argue with three mounted men. The coach laboured to a halt with a wooden groan, steam rising from the horses.

Joshua swung down and approached the door. His glove slipped on the iron, slick with ice; he caught himself, steadied, and wrenched open the door.

Barnaby Tremaine lay inside in disarray—coat skewed, cravat crushed—blinking at the burst of cold as though his rest had been disturbed.

"Fielding," he rasped. He looked inebriated and disoriented.

Joshua did not answer. His gaze had already dropped to Tremaine's boots. A length of rope—damp, frayed, unmistakable—ran from the door-stanchion around both ankles in a stout figure-of-eight, the knot hauled viciously tight. A second turn had been jammed under the seat-iron and knotted to bite at every jolt. The floor showed a smear of half-melted snow where someone had come and gone at speed. The opposite cushion bore no occupant, only the ghost of another passenger.

He reached in and flicked the rope with a gloved finger; it twanged like a plucked string.

"By all that is holy…she tied you up and escaped?"

Lord Bruton shouldered forward. One look was enough to harden his face to iron. "Where is the young lady?"

Tremaine's laugh broke on the edges. "She—tied me up!" he panted, colour mottling his cheeks. "Ungrateful—" He jerked a bound foot and hissed as the knot bit.

Joshua grabbed him by the collar. "Would you care to rethink those words?"

"She is out in this weather?" Roxton glanced at the whitening hedges, the wind sharpening the flakes to needles.

Joshua turned a fraction. "Driver—when did you take up this coach?"

"Just nigh two miles back, sir," the man muttered, his gaze sliding sideways. "Slow goin' in the storm. Gen'leman said no stoppin'."

Joshua's hand went methodically through corners and panels—no ribbon, no glove, no pin. Only the damp rope, the slush-mark, the cold draught along the inside where a window had once been forced an inch and then shoved home again.

"Where is she?" Bruton asked a second time, in a quieter tone, the question as cold as the night around them.

Tremaine's mouth worked, but hauteur deserted him. "I—did not know—" He shut his eyes as if darkness might hide his sins.

Joshua untied him from the doorpost. Tremaine sagged back and threw an arm across his face. "God help me," he said thickly into his palm.

"God help you later," Bruton said. "For now—out."

Joshua cut the second knot with one clean pull of his knife, and Tremaine yelped as blood woke in his feet. Between them, they hauled him to the verge with firm, unceremonious movements. The team stamped and blew as snow webbed the leather harness, while the wind took the open door and slammed it.

Roxton turned on his heel. "We separate now, I think. I will head back towards Wychwood. Bruton—"

"I will deal with him," Bruton said grimly. "I will not have him turn another wheel to-night." He gave the coachman a level look that emptied the man's lungs. "Back to the last inn. I will ride behind. If the lamps so much as sway oddly, I shall notice, Barnaby."

Joshua gathered Brutus' reins. "I will keep to the London road and check every cart, inn, and house. She cannot have gone far."

"Agreed," Roxton said. He gripped Joshua's forearm hard, then Bruton's. "Send word quickly if you find her, and I shall do the same."

The wind lifted a handful of snow and flung it across their faces. In that white breath, they parted. Roxton wheeled his hunter, Lord Bruton remounted and waited for the coach to turn about, and Joshua swung into the saddle and rode Brutus away from the others.

The snow thickened to a veil that swallowed the world, and Joshua pressed on, head bent, his breath clouding before him. Every few yards, he called Merry's name, the sound swallowed almost at once by the wind. Brutus's hooves made dull thuds, muffled under gathering drifts, and the hedgerows loomed like ghosts at the edge of his sight.

He stopped at the first farmstead he came to—a square of yellow light behind shuttered windows. A dog barked, shrill and distrustful, until a man's voice hushed it. When Joshua called out, the door opened a crack, spilling lamplight and the scent of wood smoke.

"Beg pardon," Joshua said, his voice rough from the cold. "Have you seen a young lady upon the road? She may be afoot—perhaps seeking help?"

The farmer shook his head, blinking at the snow. "Not a soul all night. You are the first fool I 'ave seen abroad since the storm came up."

Joshua nodded, tipped his hat in thanks, and rode on.

At the next cottage he learned nothing either. At a wayside inn, the keeper leaned in his doorway, pipe smoke curling blue about his head. "No young lady here," he said, then quickly closed the door.

Joshua spurred on, his heart thudding and his eyes narrowed against the sting of wind. Snow filled the tracks faster than horses could make them. The road became a pale blur, and the thought of Merry out in this dreadful weather kept him going forward. Now and again, he dismounted to check some mark—broken brambles, a smear where something had fallen—but the wind erased his evidence faster than he could gather it.

"Merry!" he called again, his voice muffled by the snow. Only the echo answered him, soft and useless.

Then, at a bend where the road forked, he saw a pair of wheel ruts diverging into a farm lane. Not carriage wheels—too narrow, too shallow—but those of a smaller cart, turned recently enough that the edges still glistened dark beneath their new frosting. Joshua dismounted and walked Brutus down the lane. The snow here lay deep and soft, muffling sound. A faint glow shone ahead—a lantern swinging slowly.

He came upon the slow-moving cart. The driver's head was down, his shoulders broad in a coarse smock. He straightened sharply when Joshua called out.

"Evening," Joshua said. "Have you seen a lady on the road? She may be lost or hurt."

The man's eyes flicked toward the cart behind him. "No lady," he said quickly. "Only me and the horse, sir."

Joshua's gaze followed his. The cart bed was heaped with blankets —more than a man needed for any load. Beneath the top layer, something stirred.

"'Tis a strange night to be hauling an empty cart," Joshua remarked mildly.

The man scowled. "I be on my way home now."

Joshua was about to reply when a voice rose from beneath the blankets—thin, trembling, but unmistakable. "Captain Fielding?"

He strode forward, brushing aside the top blanket. Merry's pale face blinked up at him from a nest of rough sacking and wool. Her lips were blue, her curls damp with melted snow. "Thank God you found me," she whispered, a small, shaky smile flickering through her exhaustion.

Joshua could not speak for a moment. His throat closed with something sharp and overwhelming—relief, disbelief and gratitude all at once. "You *have* given us a scare," he managed finally, his voice low and even.

"So this ain't the one what took you?" the farmer asked.

"No." She shook her head viciously. "He is family."

"I found her in the hedge, poor mite," he said briskly. "Fell from a carriage, she said, and near froze to death, so I bundled her in with the horse blankets, and was taking her to my wife."

"You have my thanks," Joshua said simply.

"The house is just there, up the lane."

Joshua helped Merry back into the cart and, leading Brutus, he followed it to the house.

The farmer opened the door and told his wife what had happened and then led the horses to a barn.

"Let us warm her by the fire before you take her anywhere," the woman ordered, already bustling them inside. "Come in, both of you. No one rides far in this weather without wishing for death to come a-calling."

Inside the low-beamed kitchen, the heat of the fireplace hit like a physical blow. The flames crackled, soup simmered, and the smell of bread and onions filled the air. Within a very few minutes, Merry sat close to the hearth, her fingers wrapped around a bowl of soup the farmer's wife had pressed upon her. Her face soon thawed to colour again, the blue fading from her lips. Once assured that Merry would do, Joshua allowed himself to be cossetted by the farmer's wife. Cold outer garments were removed, he was wrapped in warm blankets and sat by the fire with soup in hand.

"You are not hurt?" he asked softly.

"Only bruised—and very cold," she said, through chattering teeth. Her smile, faint but steady, made something inside him tighten. "I climbed out while he slept…and jumped when the carriage slowed. I had to, Joshua. He, he…" She turned away.

"You were very brave," Joshua said. "You did what needed to be done." He chuckled. "You rescued yourself."

She looked down at her bowl. "I suppose I did."

The farmer's wife glanced between them, smiling. "You will not go tonight, I hope. Snow's near blinding."

Joshua glanced at Merry, then shook his head. "My family is searching," he said. "If we do not return soon, they will be half mad with worry."

The woman clucked her tongue. "Then we will see you wrapped like parcels. There's blankets to spare."

By the time they left, the storm had eased to a whisper. The farmer and his wife stood in the doorway, lanterns casting a gold halo through the snow. Merry was wrapped in two thick cloaks, her hair tucked under a shawl, her eyes bright against her pale skin.

Joshua lifted her carefully into the saddle before him, settling her against his chest. She was trembling still, though whether from cold or from the long strain of the day, he could not tell. "You will be warmer this way," he said quietly. "Hold on to me."

She did. He felt her relax back against him, and he tucked his greatcoat about her as best he could. He let Brutus go at a steady, careful pace, the snow crunching softly beneath his tread. The wind had gentled and stars pricked faintly through the thinning clouds. It was as if the heavens had settled again now she was safe.

Merry's head rested lightly against his shoulder. "You came," she murmured, as though it surprised her.

"I will always come for you," Joshua replied, and he meant it.

They rode in silence after that, save for the steady rhythm of Brutus's hooves. Now and again, Joshua looked down at the top of her head—at the loose curl that had escaped her shawl, at the way her lashes brushed her cheek. He thought of Tremaine—drunk, craven, deceitful—and of this woman who had freed herself with rope-burned hands and a will stronger than reason.

He tightened his arm a fraction, not to claim her, only to anchor her closer against the cold.

If only, he thought, if only it had been he who had asked for her hand instead of that entitled fool. She stirred faintly, sighing against him, and he bent his head, letting her warmth sink through the layers of wool, silence and snow. The relief of having her safe settled upon him like a mantle of happiness.

When warmth and motion returned enough for thought to take shape, Merry tried to speak. Her words jostled against each other, clumsy with cold and shame.

"I am a fool," she began against the wool of Joshua's coat. "I ought to have realized—"

Her voice faltered with the admission between them. Joshua's arm tightened just slightly, enough that she could feel the steadiness of him—his breathing even, his heartbeat slow and certain beneath the layers of cloth. There was something unspoken in that silence, the kind that exists only between those who have come through a darkness together and still found each other on the other side.

In another life, she thought, he might have spoken of such things to a fellow officer over a campfire—the strange kinship of those who had walked through fear and survived it. Then, as if hearing her thoughts, Joshua murmured, half to himself, "It is like war, you know. You do not forget the ones who stand beside you when you are going through hell."

"I feared not for losing my life, but for what I was losing. I hope you can forgive—"

"Hush," he said, very gently, without censure. "There is nothing to forgive." His arm drew the blanket closer about her shoulders. "You are safe. That is all the talking needed now."

She subsided. It was surprising how easily the burden shifted when told…when one was safe. The steady beat of Brutus's stride, the measured rise and fall of Joshua's breathing, made a cradle of safety. She must have dozed, for the next she knew the world had opened into lamps and voices and the arch of Wychwood's great door flung wide like a held breath set free.

She woke as the horse checked and Joshua's arm tightened to steady her. For an instant she did not know where her body ended and began. Then the reality of the house, glowing against the snow, put its stamp upon the moment. She had fallen asleep in Joshua's arms —and nothing about it felt wrong. It was, rather, as if 'twas where she belonged. It is easy to know the shape of rightness once one has been shown its opposite. Barnaby had taught her that much, in the unkind way of lessons one does not ask for.

If only it had been Joshua who had asked for her hand, she thought in one treacherous streak before the clamour of welcome swept all such thoughts to a distant corner.

It seemed the entire household had been watching for them. Lanterns bobbed in the drive, figures hurried across the flags, and the hall beyond was peopled to its furthest shadow. Merry could not tell, at first, who belonged to Roxton and who to Fielding—the two families were so interwoven that their grief and rejoicing wore the same faces.

"Thank God!" her mother's voice exclaimed—and then everything dissolved into a purposeful flurry. Joshua dismounted and slid her down into his arms, then contrived to carry her inside and set her down without surrendering an inch of protection.

She thought she would be spared at least ten seconds before the fuss began. She was not. Her wet cloak was eased from her shoulders; snow shaken carefully from her hair; questions asked and answers not waited for. The relief of so many beloved faces was a force that had nowhere to spend itself but in action.

"I can walk," she protested faintly, finding it necessary to assert herself in some manner.

"Of course you can," Mrs. Fielding said with brisk tenderness. "You shall practise on the morrow. For tonight we shall indulge you with a bath, tea, and being wrapped up near the fire."

The Fielding brothers and Mr. Lennox had returned from their search not half an hour before, having decided she had not travelled north. Some of the flustering was spared her and transferred to them.

"Mama," Merry said, and her mother's arms closed about her with a restraint that made it stronger. Mrs. Roxton did not weep. She breathed, "My love," against Merry's hair as a blessing.

Merry wished, for a moment, that she were back within Joshua's protective circle. It was absurd to feel at once so cosseted and exposed. Affection, when poured by many at once, can feel like a bath drawn a degree too hot. Joshua, she saw, had retreated a half-step, far enough to give the women their space. Their eyes met, and the ribbon of panic that had been coiled just under her ribs loosened.

"You will not be ill, will you?" Penelope whispered, crouching at her knee like a girl rather than a married elder sister. "Say you will not be ill."

"I will not be ill," Merry said, and smiled with the relief of being permitted a joke.

Voices fluttered around them like dry leaves. The sound made her giddy with gratitude. She sipped her tea obediently. Heat slipped down to the places that had gone cold and thoughtful.

"Lord Bruton?" Joshua's father asked him, leaning one shoulder against the doorpost, the question spare and precise.

"Has his son," Joshua answered. He did not elaborate. A line of weariness around his mouth said enough about the remainder.

His father gave a brusque nod, indicating the answer to be enough.

Mrs Fielding laid a hand on Merry's shoulder and offered nothing but touch. It was enough to hold the next rush of tears at bay.

"Can you tell us—?" Mrs. Roxton began.

"Later, Mama," Merry said, a little too quickly.

"Very well," her mother returned. "Later. Come upstairs, dearest. A bath should be prepared by now."

In her chamber, steam and soap turned the world from chaos to order. Merry endured being undressed like a child and washed like a dowager, grateful to be told what to do by women who loved her enough not to ask whether she wished it. The hot water stung her rope-burns. Her hair was coaxed into civility; her wounds were dressed. She was tucked into a night-rail and a warmed wrapper and then into bed with warm bricks and a roaring fire flickering in the grate. She thought she would sleep at once. However, once alone, memories intruded.

Merry lay still under the weight of clean linens and tried not to relive the last twenty-four hours. Tremaine's betrayal—the rope—the fear—being chilled to the bone. Then, of course it was the brave, gallant Captain Fielding who would ride to her rescue. The relief at hearing his voice and realizing he was her saviour… The particular feel of his coat under her cheek, and of his arms around her as if she had been something precious and hard-won. No recriminations came from his lips, only strength and reassurance.

A tap at the door saved her from that dangerous pathway of thought. Penelope slid in sideways as if she were not a full-grown woman but a conspirator in a nursery.

"I shall be only a minute," she whispered. "Mama said you must not talk—so I came to talk."

"Sit down, then," Merry said, suppressing a smile. "Whisper at once."

Penelope perched on the bed. "I wanted only to say you need not be ashamed. People—" She waved a hand to include all of creation. "—have made a religion of pretending women are to blame for men's sins. We will stand by you no matter what is said. That is the entirety of my sermon. How are your hands?"

"They sting."

Penelope's expression softened into something fierce. "What a horrible human he turned out to be. None of it was your fault."

Merry reached and squeezed her sister's fingers. "How grateful I am for you."

"Likewise." Penelope kissed her quickly on the brow and vanished with the efficiency of a smuggler. Merry was wiping away tears when the door opened a second time.

It was Joshua. He halted at once, as if the threshold might mislike gentlemen past midnight. Mama must have sanctioned the visit. *One does not slip past that garrison*, Merry reflected, though it hardly mattered now.

He looked larger in the small light, and gentler. His hair was wet from his own bath and he was in fresh clothing but down to his shirt sleeves. The sight was absurdly moving.

"I promised two minutes," he said, his voice low. "May I squander them?"

"Please," she answered, and sat up, the pillows rearranging themselves dutifully about her shoulders.

He came no nearer than the chair by the hearth. Even that felt daring. He set his forearms to his knees, hands loose, as men do when they speak without armour.

"Joshua—" She heard the plea in it and disapproved of its nakedness. She tried again. "I am grateful beyond anything I can—"

"You must be grateful to a farmer," he returned. "As for me—" His gaze dropped to her bandaged hands. "You did the difficult thing yourself."

"I climbed out of a moving carriage like an idiot," she said, attempting levity and failing. The corners of her mouth betrayed her. She looked at him fully then. "I knew you would come."

Something changed within that moment.

His breath dipped a fraction. "I am surer of finding a road in snow than most men," he answered.

Of course he would minimize his efforts. Courage, like warmth, seemed to return in little waves. "You are hurt nowhere?" she asked.

"Only my pride," he said solemnly. "I had thought to prevent this folly."

"It was my folly," she insisted. "Had I listened to you sooner instead of my own pride…"

"I only want what is best for you, Merry." Colour touched his cheekbones and vanished. He rose, as if he had said too much. "I shall see you in the morning," he said.

"Good night, Captain," she said, more formally than her heart intended.

He stood, and then, on some private impulse, took two steps nearer and reached for her blanket. He drew it an inch higher at the shoulder and tucked her in. His fingers brushed her shoulders, but she felt it to her toes. Then he kissed the top of her head and left.

When he had gone, the air he had warmed by standing in it cooled at once. She lay back and stared at the ceiling's fine cracks and the shadows of holly pricked soft along the cornice. Exhaustion came at her from both ends—mind and body—but still her mind wondered. Could he forgive her stupidity? Could he see her as more than a silly little sister?

CHAPTER 15

The final days of Christmas-tide were always quieter. The music and laughter had thinned like the embers of the Yule fire, glowing still but softer now, more golden than bright. The holly wreaths had begun to crisp at the edges, and the evergreen boughs above the doors gave off a drier, sharper scent. In another day or two, the world would right itself from its brief season of magic and go on into the new year.

Joshua had always found this part of the season hardest—the moment between warmth and departure, when joy still lingered but farewell already waited at the door. This year, that ache was keener than before. He had begun to dread leaving Wychwood altogether.

Each morning since Merry's rescue, the thought of London tugged at him less as a summons and more as a loss waiting to happen. The capital would seem dull and spiritless after this—after her.

He had not seen much of Merry since they'd returned that night. She had been surrounded by the women of both families—their compassion as smothering as it was well meant. Her mother and sister had scarcely let her out of their sight. His mother had taken to sitting beside her during tea, watching her with that mixture of maternal pride and concern women reserve for daughters not their own.

Merry's quietness had alarmed them all, though Joshua thought it no more than exhaustion—the kind of stillness that comes after fear, when one's body remembers safety but one's mind is slower to trust it.

The talk in the village, though, had been less kind. He had overheard it himself at the tavern that morning—two old farmers at the counter, a washerwoman by the door. All had opinions about Miss Roxton.

"Poor lass," one had said. "She's been led astray, she has."

"She's lucky the family has stood by her," said another. "The outcome could have been much worse. That Tremaine fellow is a blackguard."

Then, however, came the undertone Joshua had expected and dreaded—the whisper that travelled under every woman's name once rumour caught hold.

"They say she was half taken in by him, though," the washerwoman murmured. "It weren't all force, I'll wager."

Joshua had left his ale untouched and gone out before he said something that would be remembered.

Those who had known Merry all her life—the tenants, the tradesmen, the servants—would stand by her, of that he was sure. They knew her temper, her kindness, her impossible honesty. Yet others would not. To some, the story would shrink to a single dangerous thread—a young lady who had looked too high and forgotten herself. The same mouths that had praised her beauty would purse in disapproval now that she had become an item of gossip.

Joshua clenched his jaw at the thought. It was no fault of hers that she had been deceived; no sin that she had trusted charm over character. Tremaine's villainy was his own, and his punishment just, but the world rarely divided guilt so cleanly.

He would marry her if she would have him. The decision had shaped itself days ago, though he had not yet spoken it aloud. He could give her protection and peace, and perhaps, in time, something like joy. They dealt well together—that much he knew. She met him without artifice or fear, and she made him laugh when nothing else could.

And yet...

He could not be certain she wanted him. If he asked now, would she believe he offered out of pity—or guilt? She had suffered too much humiliation to bear either. Better, perhaps, that he should return to London, let time smooth the edges of her ordeal, and then—when she had rebuilt her pride—come back.

He turned that thought over all morning, his fingers worrying the coin in his pocket, until he found himself, by sheer instinct, seeking out his mother.

He found his mother in the morning room, the pale winter light falling over her embroidery frame. She was making a pattern of ribbons and holly leaves intertwined—and humming under her breath. At his step, she looked up, as sharp-eyed and calm as ever.

"Joshua," she said, setting down her work. "You have that look about you."

He smiled faintly. "Do I look as miserable as I feel, then?"

"No, dear, you look worse," she said forthrightly. "Now sit down and tell me what trouble you have made for yourself."

He obeyed, though his hands remained restless on his knees. "Not trouble, precisely," he said slowly, "but—Mother, what would you think if I told you I meant to offer for Merry?"

Mrs. Fielding's needle paused in mid-air, gleaming like a captured drop of sunlight. "What would I think?" she repeated softly. "I think it has taken you long enough to realize you were meant for each other."

"Mother—?"

"Oh, do not look so scandalized, Joshua. You have worn your heart upon your sleeve since Christmas Eve."

He laughed, a little helplessly. "Quoting Othello? You think me in love, then?"

"I think you are in turmoil," she said, "which is near enough to the same thing."

He sobered. "If I could be sure it would not harm her further, I would ask her now, but I—perhaps I should wait. Give her time. Let the village gossip fade before—"

"Oh, nonsense." Mrs Fielding waved her hand as if batting away an insect. "You gentlemen always imagine we are delicate. She will suffer more if you wait. I think she had realized Tremaine was unworthy before he ever put his hand on her arm."

Joshua exhaled. He had known that, deep down. Merry had begun to suspect Tremaine's attentions were not as honourable as she had wished. He'd seen it in the way her eyes had hardened with hurt even before the night of her abduction, when she had sent the letter to break the betrothal.

"She did know," he said quietly. "But that does not mean her heart was untouched, nor that she has room in it for me."

Mrs. Fielding looked at him for a long moment. There was a glint of amusement in her gaze, but also something warmer—maternal pride, perhaps, or simply recognition. "I know for a fact, my dear," she said at last, "that Merry has always sought your attention. She only pestered you because you were too proud to notice her."

"We were just children," he said, though the words rang weakly even to his own ears.

His mother scoffed delicately. "Children know what they like, even if they cannot name it. You were the only one she ever followed into mischief. She thought the sun rose and set by your lead."

He rubbed the back of his neck, embarrassed and oddly heartened. "Then why did she accept Tremaine?"

"Because she was out of options, my dear." Mrs. Fielding's tone softened. "A young woman of fortune may have many admirers and no freedom at all. She took the first man who seemed to offer her both admiration and escape. Do not judge her for it. In loneliness, we have all made foolish choices."

Joshua sat back, remaining silent. Could it be true? Had Merry truly looked to Tremaine out of desperation rather than affection? That seemed an insult to her spirit, yet he could not entirely dismiss it. He had seen that same restlessness in her—the yearning to belong somewhere, to be more than the spinster sister left behind when others married.

He remembered her laughter when skating, bright and infectious; then her calm at the farmhouse when she had been half-frozen and yet still tried to thank him before giving herself credit. A woman like that would not settle for pity; but love—for love she might take the risk.

Mrs. Fielding watched him, smiling a little. "You think too much," she said. "A woman's heart is not a riddle to be solved on a battlefield. Go to her. Tell her what you feel. If she refuses, at least you will have spoken the truth. It is better than silence."

"Perhaps," he said, though doubt still pricked. "But if she refuses, she will not only lose a suitor—she will lose a friend."

"Joshua," his mother said, reaching across the space to take his hand, "she will never lose that. Whatever else happens, she trusts you, and that is worth more than all the proposals in Christendom."

He smiled faintly, though the ache in his chest remained.

That evening, as the last of the daylight faded into dusk, Joshua walked up and down the terrace outside the library. From there, he could see the glow of the drawing room through the windows—the gentle chaos within. The ladies sat by the fire, their laughter softer now, the rhythm of contentment returning. Merry was there, between her sister and Mrs. Fielding, her hair loosely plaited in quiet defiance of decorum.

She looked tired, but not fragile. Her eyes were turned toward the hearth, and her smile—small, inward, half-formed—was one he'd never seen on her lips before.

Joshua stood watching until the cold crept through his gloves, then turned back toward the door.

Could his mother be right? Could it truly be that Merry's heart had looked his way all this time, and he had been too blind to see it?

He remembered her voice on the road home, half-asleep against him. 'I knew you would come.'

It had sounded like belief.

Now, as he entered the house, the warmth of the fire and the hum of laughter wrapping around him, he thought—perhaps—that belief was where love began.

Tomorrow, he would ask her. Not from pity, not from duty, but because she deserved to hear, from his own lips, what she had already proved in his heart: that she was the bravest, finest, and dearest woman he had ever known.

And if she said no—well, then he would carry her memory with him as a mark of honour, not loss of love.

He crossed to the drawing room door, and paused, just long enough to see her lift her head and glance his way, as if sensing him there.

Her eyes met his, and for the first time since that terrible night, she smiled fully—warm, unguarded and alive.

It was enough to make him hope.

And hope, Joshua thought, was as good a beginning as any.

ALAS, they had reached Twelfth Night. The greenery drooped a little lower, and the yule log, so triumphantly set on Christmas Day, was a faint glow of embers. Merriment still reigned, yet in every laugh there lurked a little ache for the morrow. Tomorrow meant trunks and wraps and farewells. It meant Joshua would be returning to London, and Merry held more sadness in her heart over that than she did for the foolishness she had imagined to exist with Barnaby.

Loss took a clearer shape now. It was not a wound that smarted with shame. It was an empty space that had discovered its size only when a certain gentleman's presence had filled it, and now threatened to be vacant again.

The great table shone with the last splendour of the season. Candles threw clear light over polished silver and bright crystal. The children occupied their saloon with a riot of puddings and giggles. Merry slid into her place and only then saw that fate, or two mothers, had organized the company to perfection. Joshua sat at her right hand.

He glanced down, humour alive in his eyes. "Our mothers are meddling again," he remarked in a voice pitched for her alone.

Merry adopted an air of patient resignation. "May I remind you it is inevitable. Does it trouble you?"

"Not at all," he said, the corner of his mouth lifting. "I need all the help I can contrive."

Before she could ask what he meant, his brother, Aaron, demanded a history of some army story from Portugal, and Joshua turned obligingly to tell it. Merry took a sip of wine and watched the easy animation with which he complied. He made attention feel like warmth.

The courses moved forward with all their ceremonious cheer. Somewhere between a dish of salmon dressed with capers and a roast of beef in Hollandaise, Merry said quietly, "I had an apology from Lord Bruton earlier."

Joshua stilled. "Did you?"

"He begged pardon without artifice. He accepted the full blame and declared himself at my disposal should I ever need anything in his power to give. The line that caught me was the last. 'I will not ask your forgiveness for my son. I ask it for myself, who saw the path he was taking and did not succeed in turning him from it.'"

Joshua considered her for a breath. "How does it make you feel?"

"I am beset by sadness," she said. "Sadness that a gentleman like him has such an undeserving son. I believe he meant to do better and could not."

His gaze softened. "Your graciousness does you credit."

"I do not feel gracious," she said, setting down her fork. "I feel tired of being angry at Tremaine, and more so at myself. Anger is rather a heavy burden to carry."

He paused, and in that single pause she felt a conversation grow between them that no one else could hear. It lay there in the quiet as if it had always been waiting and had at last found voice.

They were not left to it for long. Twelfth Night refused to be solemn. The Fieldings welcomed several village families as the dishes were cleared, the room filling at once with the good noise of neighbours. Mr. and Mrs. Finch came from the mill; old Mr. Parkes, who had tuned the church spinet since the reign of the last vicar, arrived; and also came the vicar and his wife themselves. Scarves were unwound. Cloaks were whisked away. Boots were stamped clean in the passage. The company widened like a circle of lantern light in a winter lane.

The first set began as soon as the footmen had rolled up the carpets. Mr. Roxton took Mrs. Finch's arm with a gallantry that suited him. Mr. Lennox bowed to Mrs. Fielding. Joshua made a point of claiming little Rose and took her through the figures with such kindness that the child glowed pink and bold by the close. Someone had brought a fiddle. Someone else had a lute. The music was jovial.

Merry stood a little apart when she could. On the fringes of laughter one hears notes that do not belong to the tune. A remark, thrown away by a woman who wished to be known for saying what others would not, was levied directly into her ear.

"Well, Miss Roxton," the woman murmured behind her fan, "you will just have to remain a spinster now, I dare say. A safe choice for everyone, do you not agree, for who would take you now?"

Merry turned her head very slightly, enough to meet the woman's gaze without gifting it consequence. "A safe choice is sometimes the best," she said. "There are worse fates than being one's own responsibility."

The woman coloured and laughed as if she had meant only a jest. Merry let it pass. If that was the worst folks were saying about her, then she would endure. Joshua was on the other side of the room, speaking to the vicar, and she would not let the evening sour while she could still watch him and memorize every line of his face.

When the second country dance was called, he crossed to her as if the space belonged to his stride. "May I have this dance?" he asked, at once both formal and simple.

"You may," she said, and placed her hand in his.

They took their places. The set was lively, full of turning and pursuit and quick crossings. Merry found her feet obedient again, her breathing keeping time with the measures. Joshua's hand was sure when he took hers, assured when he let it go. Once or twice their eyes met and slid away; once or twice they held. She was astonished at the calm in her own chest. This ought to have been a moment for tremors and desperate questions. Instead it felt like standing where she was meant to be.

When the dance ended, a draught rose as someone opened the French doors to the terrace. Cold air washed the crowded room. Merry, warm and a little flushed, lifted her face to the breath of winter and smiled. Joshua saw that smile and, without ceremony, offered his arm.

"Would you care for some fresh air?" he asked.

"Yes, I should like that," she answered.

They stepped out into a world made silver by frost. The terrace stones were dry but cold. Beyond, the lawn lay smooth and pale under a sky pricked with hard stars. Their breath smoked in the lamplight. Behind them came the faint strum of the fiddler tuning for another set. For a moment they stood with the night laid open like a page before them.

"My brothers mean to take down the greenery tomorrow," Joshua said, because a gentleman must say something as he learns to be brave. "The house will look very dull."

"I admire a thing that does not pretend to be what it is not."

They walked the length of the terrace in companionable quiet. Twice she thought he would speak; twice he did not. The second time she spoke for him, not to hurry but to solve the earlier riddle. "You said our mothers were meddling."

"They did," he said with a faint smile, "and I find I am grateful to be easily managed."

They reached the end of the terrace, where a little bough of mistletoe had been tucked into the lintel. A sprig still hung there, absurd and audacious, its white berries dull in the starlight.

Merry looked up and laughed, but her laugh came out as a breath rather than a sound. He looked up too. The mischief of the thing lay between them like a delicate trap. She felt the balance of the moment shift. One step would spring it—or save it.

"Do I imagine," she said, and her voice trembled in a way that made her cross with herself, "that there is something more than there is?"

"No," he said at once. "You do not imagine."

She let out the breath she had not known she held. "Then I am not mad?"

"You are not mad."

"Only foolish," she said, attempting a smile.

"Brave," he corrected, but he did not step away when they stopped.

He stood very straight, as if he had come to attention. "Merry," he said quietly, "if I am honest, I have come to admire you greatly. I find I cannot look at a day and not wish to put you into it. You deserve someone who values you as you are, and I aspire to be that man."

She felt tears threaten, quickly rejected them, and paced once the length of their little shelter. Words poured out before she could tidy them. "I should like to explain. It may appear I am fickle. I am not. At the time, I had no hope of a better match. I thought myself already on the shelf. I thought Barnaby to be a door to a different world, and I was foolish enough to be grateful for any door that opened."

He listened without flinching, which was how a man should listen. "I might be your second choice," he said, almost lightly, "but I would offer you the protection of my name nonetheless."

She stopped and faced him. "But you are not my second choice."

He went very still. "No? There is another?"

She almost laughed then, from nervousness and joy together. "You mock me when I would lay my heart before you?"

"Indeed not," he said, and something like relief moved across his features. He took one step nearer, enough to bring the starlight into his eyes. "But I am going to kiss you now."

He raised his hands and set them to her face with a care that made them feel like a blessing. The first touch of his mouth was light. The second found its courage in the first. He kissed her as if he was learning every bit of her and wished to know by heart. It was nothing like Tremaine's cold kiss. It was steadier, warmer, and in its warmth there lay a promise—that he would not take what was not given and would treasure all that was. In fact, the two men were not comparable at all, she told herself in irritation, and she would stop thinking about that horrid man whilst Joshua's lips were upon hers.

When he drew back, he rested his forehead against hers. Their breath mingled and made a small cloud between them that broke and vanished and formed again.

"And indeed," he murmured, almost against her lips, "I will beg an answer of you since you seem to enjoy taunting me."

"Tit for tat," she said, smiling now without fear, "but I will not accept you merely for the protection of your name."

"No?" He sounded entirely ready to be improved by instruction.

"I would accept you for your heart as well, if you please, since mine already belongs to you."

He gave a sound that might have been a laugh and might have been a prayer. "I can think of no better Christmas gift."

"Happy Christmas, Joshua," she whispered, and then, remembering what he had once said, corrected herself with a little tilt of her head. "Or perhaps that should be Merry Christmas instead?"

"I shall prefer it always," he said.

Then he looked at her—really looked—and some soft restraint in his eyes gave way. He bent again and kissed her once more, longer, deeper this time, as if sealing something sacred between them. The world seemed to fall away—the cold air, the faint music drifting from the house, the snowlight trembling over the terrace. There was only the quiet thud of her heart and the steady warmth of his hands.

When at last they parted, he kept his brow resting against hers. "I love you, Merry," he said quietly, as if the words had been waiting years for air. "I believe I have for longer than I understood."

Her eyes shone with tears she did not attempt to hide. "And I, you."

Above them hung the mistletoe, its pale berries gleaming like drops of milk in the lamplight. Joshua reached up and plucked one, holding it between finger and thumb.

"There are far too many left," he said, his voice roughened with laughter and tenderness both. "It would be a pity to waste them."

"Then you must take one for every kiss owed," she answered, daring him now with a glint in her eye.

He tucked the berry into her palm, closing her fingers over it. "A token," he said, "to remind you that I am a man of my word."

She smiled up at him, her hand still enclosed in his. "Then I shall keep it close—though I suspect you will make me earn the rest."

"Indeed," he murmured, drawing her near again, "but not before Twelfth Night is through."

And with the last of the snow whispering against the terrace stones, he kissed her again beneath the mistletoe—until laughter and promise mingled on their lips, and the rest of the world could only wait.

RECIPES

From *The London School of Cookery* by John Farley, 1802 and *A Complete System of Cookery* by John Simpson, 1806

No. 18. Chocolate Biscuits. TAKE a quarter of a pound of chocolate, and put it on a tin, over a stove to make it warm, then put a pound of powdered sugar in a bason, and when the chocolate is quite warm and soft, put it in with the sugar, and mix it well with about eight whites of eggs, if you find it too thin, mix more powdered sugar with it just to bring it to a paste, so that you can roll it in lumps as big as walnuts: let your oven be moderate, put three papers under them, let the oven just raise them and make them crisp and firm, and let them be quite cold before you take them off the paper.

No. 22. Fine Sweetmeat Gingerbread Nuts. TAKE two pounds of the best treacle and put it in a large bason; then take half a pound of the best fresh butter, and carefully melt it, not to oil, pour the butter to the treacle, and stir it well as you pour it in; add three quarters of an ounce of the best pounded ginger, and put in with it two ounces of preserved lemon and orange peel cut very small; and two ounces of preserved angelica, likewise cut very small; and one ounce of corriander seed pounded, and one ounce and a half of carraway seeds whole, mix them well together; then break two eggs, yolks and whites together, and mix as much flour as will bring it to a fine paste; make them the size you choose; put them on the bare tin plate, and let your oven be rather brisk.

No. 35. Fine Ginger Cakes. TAKE four pounds of flour, and put on your dresser, then take a copper saucepan, and break six eggs, and mix them well with a spoon; put one pint of cream in them, and beat them well, put the saucepan over the fire, and stir it till it is just warm; put two pounds of butter into the cream and eggs; and one pound of powdered sugar, and stir it over a very slow fire, just to melt all the butter; put in four ounces of pounded ginger, and when all the butter is melted, pour it all into the middle of the flour, mix it as well as you can, and when you have made it a fine paste, roll it out with flour under it, on your dresser, cut them to the size of the top of a breakfast cup, and a quarter of an inch thick: put three papers under them, before you put them in the oven, which must be very hot. N. B. These are very good for the stomach in cold weather.

AFTERWORD

Author's note: British spellings and grammar have been used in an effort to reflect what would have been done in the time period in which the novels are set. Yes, Jane Austen used -ize spellings, even though -ise is accepted now. While I realize all words may not be exact, I hope you can appreciate the differences and effort made to be historically accurate while attempting to retain readability for the modern audience.

Thank you for reading *A Merry Christmas.* I hope you enjoyed it. If you did, please help other readers find this book:

1. This ebook is lendable, so send it to a friend who you think might like it so she or he can discover me, too.

2. Help other people find this book by writing a review.

3. Sign up for my new releases at www.Elizabethjohnsauthor.com, so you can find out about the next book as soon as it's available.

4. Come like my Facebook page www.facebook.com/Eliza bethjohnsauthor or follow on Instagram @Ejohnsauthor or feel free to write me at elizabethjohnsauthor@gmail.com

ACKNOWLEDGMENTS

There are many, many people who have contributed to making my books possible.

My family, who deals with the idiosyncrasies of a writer's life that do not fit into a 9 to 5 work day.

Dad, who reads every single version before and after anyone else—that alone qualifies him for sainthood.

Anj, who takes my visions and interpret them, making them into works of art people open in the first place.

To those friends who care about my stories enough to help me shape them before everyone else sees them.

Heather who helps me say what I mean to!

And to the readers who make all of this possible.

I am forever grateful to you all.